Saving a Cowboy's Christmas

Rodeo Road Series: Book 3

Stephanie Berget

Other Titles by Stephanie Berget

Rodeo Road
Changing A Cowboy's Tune
Winning A Cowgirl's Heart

Sugar Coated Cowboys
Gimme Some Sugar
Sweet Cowboy Kisses
Cowboy's Sweetheart
Sugar Pine Cowboy

Harney County Cowboys
Tied To A Dream
Dancing Creek Ranch
Rocky Road Home

STEPHANIE BERGET

SAVING A COWBOY'S CHRISTMAS

It's easy to fall in love…
The hard part is finding someone to catch you.

Her daddy abandoned her without a backward glance.
Her mother wasn't any kind of safety net.

Her childhood friend was the perfect answer—kind, caring, and smoking hot. Too bad his heart is broken by his almost ex-wife, country music's newest sweetheart.

She's been a lot of things, but rebound girl isn't on her list, even for a cowboy that's always been out of her league.

But one kiss and her heart stops listening to her brain.

If you like friends-to-lovers western romance, try *Saving A Cowboy's Christmas*, because love isn't something you find. Love finds you.

STEPHANIE BERGET

DEDICATION

This book is dedicated to my parents. Although they were confirmed city people, they supported me when the most important things in my life were horses and rodeos.

They suffered through every western and horse related television show, including My Friend Flicka every Saturday morning for years. They bought me my first horse when I was fourteen and came to watch me at my rodeos and horse shows, encouraging my passion.

Later, when I started writing, they were thrilled to read what I'd written.

Thanks, Mom and Dad.

You were the best!

STEPHANIE BERGET

CHAPTER ONE

Black plastic exploded in tiny shards as Drew's cell phone smashed into the flowered wallpaper in his Nana Lucy's living room. Glass shattered and miniscule electronic parts peppered the hardwood floor, echoing his anger. The destruction did nothing to calm him.

After six years of marriage, his wife had kicked him to the curb. With her country music career soaring toward the stars, he wasn't country enough for her anymore.

Drew Dunbar, a man who'd been raised on a ranch, and had spent years managing her career, was suddenly persona non grata.

He sank onto his grandmother's couch and covered his head with his hands.

To be honest, he'd known something was wrong when Abbie hadn't made it home to sing at his brother Davie's wedding, but he hadn't wanted to face the facts. He'd been in love with the beautiful blonde in one form or another since they'd been fourteen. When she'd grown more distant, he'd assumed she was tired from all the touring.

Looking back, although he had no concrete proof, he'd bet the ranch she'd been sleeping with her producer, the fabulous Mitchell, for months.

At the soft sounds of Nana Lucy moving around the kitchen, he gathered his anger and hid it in a corner of his soul.

Grabbing his cap, he jammed it on his head and snuck out the front door. As he shoved the gearshift into first on the Porsche Cayman sports car he'd bought for Abbie two months ago, his grandmother stepped out the door, waving to get his attention. She held parts of the broken phone in her hand.

Not now, and probably not ever, would he feel right discussing this with Nana Lucy. He waved and hit the gas. Even if he hadn't fooled her with the wave, she'd have time to get over her anger by the time he got back.

If he came back.

The urge to hit the road was strong. He could drive away from all his problems and start a new life. Only one thing kept that from happening. The phone call he'd received was from Abbie's lawyer. The man wanted to let him know there would be no splitting of assets. The woman he'd married believed any money earned during their marriage belonged to her. The only way he'd get what was his was to fight her in court.

As he hit a straight stretch on Highway 95, he shifted again and stomped on the gas pedal. The engine screamed, and the car flew down the pavement like a coyote after a plump jackrabbit.

He'd just started to slow down for the upcoming curve when a forked-horn mule deer jumped from the sagebrush at the edge of the road into his path. Drew hit the brakes and jerked the wheel to miss the animal. By inches, the car avoided hitting the buck.

Unfortunately, Drew wasn't so lucky when it came to the speed limit sign. The post splintered close to the ground, and the sign slammed into the windshield then scraped along the top.

When the car finally came to a stop, Drew's white-knuckled hands gripped the steering wheel. After peeling his fingers loose, he reached up and turned off the engine. Silence and dust settled over the car. If he hadn't known he was the bad luck Dunbar brother before, this clinched it.

He climbed out to assess the damage.

A crazy web of cracks ran across the windshield, a three-inch dent marred the shiny red paint of the hood, and a long scrape ran the length of the top. Even though he'd put up a hefty down payment, he still owed over thirty-five thousand on the car. And, he didn't even like driving the cramped little thing.

Abbie was the one who loved it. And what Abbie coveted, Abbie got.

Leaning in the driver's door, he fished his cell phone out of the console. "Damn it." The console was empty, the phone in pieces in his grandmother's living room. He couldn't get a break if he'd won one in a raffle.

After looking first up then down the highway, Drew gave up and sank to the ground. He stretched his legs out in front of him and leaned against the tire. "Just call me Mr. Lucky," he said with a snort.

The only thing that had gone right was the weather. Indian summer was in full bloom, and though it was the middle of September, the sun was unseasonably warm, and the breeze was perfect.

He closed his eyes and imagined lying on a tropical beach. One with no cattle, and especially, no country music.

The sound of a diesel engine woke him from his reverie. An older Ford pickup, pulling a flatbed trailer, slowed then pulled off to the side of the highway in front of his car.

A tall woman dressed in dirty jeans, a Harley T-shirt, and worn work boots climbed from the cab. The way her hips swayed as she walked caught his attention for a moment. Just in time, he jerked his gaze up to her face.

Drew had known someone would stop. This was ranch

country, and everyone helped a neighbor, or even a stranger in need. As he rose, it took him a moment to recognize Gina Wallace. They hadn't spoken since he'd graduated except for a brief, uncomfortable conversation at Davie and Randi's wedding.

She closed the distance between them until her shadow blocked out the setting sun. "Get tired of driving?"

"Yeah, I thought I needed a break." Wisps of hair that had escaped her usual braid framed her face and nearly glowed in the sunlight. He didn't remember her hair being this rich honey gold.

"If you're coming from the ranch, you've driven all of ten miles. I can see why you'd need to rest up before continuing to town." Gina moved past him and leaned on the hood, assessing the damage. "I wouldn't have thought a little sign like that could do all this damage."

"Only to me and only with this expensive piece of ego inflation." Drew dusted off the back of his jeans and moved closer. "I was going to call a tow truck, but I forgot my phone. Can I borrow yours?" It was a little white lie, but he'd played it straight his whole life, and it hadn't done him any good. Maybe he'd try fabricating the truth for a while.

"I can do better than that. See the trailer?" She waved her hand in the direction of the rig. "I can take you wherever you want to go."

"How about Bali?" Drew forced a smile.

"Maybe I spoke too soon. My truck doesn't do well underwater." Her smile was real this time, and it lit up her face.

As he watched her, he took in her high cheekbones and long legs. When her smile faded, he realized he'd been staring. "I'd appreciate a lift. If you can take me back to the ranch, I'll haul the car into town tomorrow. I don't want to waste any more of your time."

"I dropped off the used baler John Corcoran bought so I'm off for the rest of the day, and I've got more time than

I want right now. It's no problem to haul you into town."

When she raised her gaze to his, Drew got lost for a moment in her blue eyes. They were the same shade as Abbie's but filled with something different. Maybe integrity? Definitely not unbridled ambition.

Her hair was the same as his almost ex's natural color, too, when Abbie wasn't trying out something new. That was where the similarity ended.

Abbie could have been a runway model with her exotic eyes and too wide mouth. Gina was plainer but pretty in a down home way. Someone who might be a friend. He'd had one kiss from that country girl mouth way back in high school and had never forgotten.

"If you're sure." Drew opened the driver's door and pulled out his jacket, wallet, and his hat. "The body shop will cost me a fortune, but I can't sell it until it's fixed."

"The famous Abbie Angelica is going to let you sell her car?" Gina stood with her arms crossed, watching him closely. "I thought this was her baby, or has she found another, more expensive model?" She stopped and studied him for a moment. "Sorry, did I say that out loud?"

Drew waved away the apology. "She found another model all right, but he has nothing to do with a car." He pulled in a deep breath and tried to let go of the overwhelming anger. "Unless she's conned him into buying one for her, too."

Without another word, Gina strode back to the truck, and maneuvered the rig into place in front of the Porsche before lowering the trailer ramps.

Drew fired up the engine and with care, drove onto the trailer. After putting the car in park and setting the brake, he jumped to the ground and climbed into the passenger seat. "Thanks again for doing this. I owe you."

A shy smile lit Gina's face. "Yes, you do and don't think I'll forget." She shifted into gear and headed toward Homedale.

The silence as they drove felt suffocating to Drew, but

Gina didn't seem to mind. After a few miles, he began to wonder if she'd forgotten he was here.

She softly hummed the old Rolling Stones hit, Satisfaction.

Drew sank back into his seat. He hadn't had any satisfaction since the first year he'd been married to Abbie. Of course, she'd been Abigail Beaker then, not country music's sweetheart.

"You don't like Abbie very much, do you?" Drew watched her as she drove the winding road through the desert hills.

"I'm not sure you want to know what I think of your wife." Gina snickered. "I will say this. She has the voice of a songbird." She slowed as they entered a canyon. At the first wide spot in the road, she pulled over. Leaning back against the door, she crossed her arms and gave him a glare that looked right into his soul. "What's going on?"

"You don't want to hear my sad story."

"Can't be worse than mine. Everyone in the county knew my mother didn't want me. Still doesn't."

Her tone was matter of fact, but Drew knew that kind of hurt never went away.

"And she didn't want my baby either."

There'd been a rumor that Gina was pregnant her junior year, but as a recent high school graduate, he was on to bigger and better things. "Your baby?"

"Mama didn't want her, and the only way the father offered to help was to pay for an abortion."

"I'm sorry, Gina. I didn't know." He almost asked who the father was but cut short the thought. He had enough problems of his own without asking for more.

A breeze picked up and the wisps of hair fluttered around her face. She lifted her hand to shade her eyes. "Mama said giving her up was for the best."

The baby had been a girl. "Where is she now?" Drew turned to face her. He hadn't known more than rumors about a baby, and he tried not to give credence to gossip.

"With a really nice family. Somewhere she'll always know she's loved."

Drew had known this woman most of his life but hadn't known about the most important things. "I didn't have to worry about an unwanted child. Having a baby is the last thing Abbie would put up with." He climbed out of the truck and walked to the edge of the pavement. Rounded hills tumbled to meet the valley floor, and the landscape glowed with the soft yellows and grays of the Oregon desert. He stuffed his hands in his pockets to keep from choking an imaginary Abbie.

A soft voice from behind him brought him out of his terrible memories.

"They say it helps if you tell someone." Gina stood beside him, mimicking his stance.

"Well, bullying didn't seem to work with your baby's father, and it didn't work for me." His thoughts raced back to that night two months ago, but he kept his gaze on the valley below.

Gina punched him in the arm.

He jerked his attention to the woman beside him. "Ow! What was that for?"

"You tried to get Abbie to get rid of your baby? I'm beginning to think all men are jerks." She turned and strode back to the truck. The engine fired up, but the one-ton didn't pull away leaving him on the mountain.

Worried she'd change her mind, Drew hurried to the pickup. He climbed in but kept his gaze fixed out the window. "You've got this wrong. I tried to talk her into having the baby. She wasn't interested, and she took care of her problem before even telling me. Turns out it was probably for the best. She's found a guy she thinks will help her career, and a baby would have gotten in the way."

***

Gina studied the cowboy slumped in the passenger seat

of her battered pickup. With his starched Wranglers, pressed western shirt, and black cowboy hat, Drew was the epitome of the man she'd pick if she believed in men anymore.

She shook her head in an attempt to clear her mind. It was obvious his feelings about the abortion were still raw. Besides, she'd given up her cowboy dream long ago. "I'm sorry, Drew."

"Yeah, everybody will be sorry when they find out, except Abbie. She's ecstatic." He raised his gaze to meet her eyes, sadness filling his expression. "Don't tell anyone yet. I can't take their pity."

Shifting into gear, she pulled onto the road toward town. As they dropped into the valley, the highway became one sharp curve after another. Gina was forced to keep her eyes on the road, but her mind couldn't let go of what he'd said.

This wasn't any of her business, and a smart woman would keep her mouth shut, but she'd proved time and time again, she wasn't a smart woman. "I can guarantee you what I feel isn't pity."

Drew was a good man. From what she'd heard, he'd done everything Abbie had ever asked. Now was the time to shut up. She'd said enough.

"Really?" The sarcasm in his voice caught her attention. "What about sympathy, or disappointment, or thinking I'm a fool? They're all the same. Right now, I'm the biggest sucker in the country." He slumped even lower.

She was stuck her nose farther into this subject than she should. Might as well dive in headfirst. "What I feel is anger. Abbie is a spoiled brat, and someday she's going to regret her actions. I hope you don't take her back. She's a user, Drew. Even in Junior High, manipulation was always her go-to plan."

Drew lifted his cap and ran one hand through his hair. He gave a humorless chuckle. "Don't hold back, Wally. Tell me how you really feel."

"Only if you stop calling me Wally. That was my Dad's pet name. I didn't like it when I was little, and I don't like it now." Stepping on the brake, she pulled up to the stop sign then turned toward Homedale.

What the hell was she thinking? She'd been told many times over she should learn to back off. Easier said than done for a Wallace. No matter how hard she tried, her mouth took control of her brain. In an effort to change the subject, she asked, "What are your plans? Are you staying on the ranch?"

Drew hadn't been at the ranch for more than a few days at a time since he'd married the singer. That's how Gina thought of Drew's wife—the singer. Because in Gina's view, a voice was all she was.

"Don't know." Drew shook his head. "I don't really have anywhere else to go. I don't want to be a bother to my brothers and their wives. I wasn't around when the old man needed me, or when Dex had to run the ranch after Dad died. I'm pretty sure they aren't interested in me coming home now."

Gina knew how that felt. She'd always been a bother to her family and the odd man out with her classmates. "I don't believe they'd kick you out, besides you must have other options. What about the music business?"

"I haven't done anything but be Abbie's manager. I'd have to convince the music world that I wasn't just the talent's husband." His arms wrapped around himself as if to ward off thoughts of Abbie. "And that's hard in a business where the only important thing is what you've done lately."

"It sounds to me like you didn't enjoy the country music world. Maybe it's time for you to come home and figure out who Drew Dunbar is." Gina turned into Mike's Auto Repair and stopped the truck. "You never know. You might find out you like the man."

"You never know." Drew managed what looked like a genuine smile. "Let's go see if Mike can fix this hunk of

17

junk."

"I've got an errand to run. You go talk to Mike, and I'll be back in a few minutes." Gina grabbed the white envelope from the dash and walked across the street to the bank.

"How's your day going, Gina?" Mary King, her one-time neighbor, stood behind the counter. She'd taken the tellers job right after college.

"Not too bad. I finally got the tractor salvage to pay me what they owed me. I might even be able to afford a burger for dinner. Big night out." Gina signed the check and slid it across the polished surface.

Mary grinned and leaned forward. "I wasn't going to say anything, but isn't that Drew I saw you with? I didn't know he was back in town."

"I helped haul his car in to be repaired." Gina tapped her short nails on the counter then stuffed them into her pockets. Unlike Mary's manicured nails, hers were dirty. "I'm kind of in a hurry. Things to do, you know."

Mary counted out the cash Gina had kept then handed her the receipt for the deposit. "What I wouldn't do to find a way to get rid of Abbie for a while. In my opinion, Drew is by far the cutest of the Dunbar brothers."

"Since all the brothers are married, you'd be better off doing your job and not lusting after someone you can't have."

Mary blushed and gasped as Gina took a step back. Her brows drew down. Her lips thinned into a sharp line. "Oh, I get it." The teller glanced around, probably hoping to find someone to side with her. "You couldn't get Dex or Davie so you want Drew for yourself. I hate to tell you this, Gina, but you don't have a chance against Abbie. She's so sweet and pretty, and you got knocked up and gave your baby away."

What Gina wanted to do and what she did do were two different things. She pulled in a breath and let it out slowly. "Thanks for your help, Mary." Turning on her heel, she sauntered out of the bank, her heart pounding. No doubt most of the town would have the same opinion, especially when they found out Drew and Abbie were having problems.

Gina had had a crush on Dex in middle school. Even at that young age, he'd never noticed anyone but Mavis. So, Dex and Mavis had become her buddies.

She'd never thought of Davie as more than a crazy friend. Too bad no one would believe that story.

Drew, she hadn't thought of much at all. Although, he was only one year older than she was, and he'd hung around when he hadn't been off with his own friends, they hadn't been close.

She could see Drew talking to the mechanic through the dusty plate glass window in the front of the Auto Repair. Shifting her gaze to the car, she shook her head. It was going to cost more than she made in a year to fix that thing. Movement caught her attention as Drew and Mike came out to the trailer.

Drew backed the Porsche to the ground and pulled it into the mechanic's bay. He shook Mike's hand then hurried across the road. "Can I buy you dinner to repay you?"

Before she could answer, Mary came out the bank door and nearly shouldered Gina out of her way to stand in front of Drew. "Drew, it's so nice to see you again." Leaning closer to him, the woman shot a short glance toward Gina before continuing. "A word of advice. Be careful of the company you keep." With a wave, the teller climbed into her car and drove away.

"What's her problem?" Drew shifted his gaze from the retreating car to Gina, his brows pulled into a frown.

"Apparently, she thinks you and I are an item, and she's not happy about that." Gina stepped into the street before turning back to Drew. "I'm starved. Want to get a burger?"

STEPHANIE BERGET

CHAPTER TWO

The chorus to Blake Shelton's "Goodbye Time" rang out in the early morning air. When Drew answered, the voice on the other end had a slick, professional tone.

"Mr. Dunbar, I'm calling from Michael Parker's office. Can you hold for Mr. Parker?"

"Sure." Drew walked into the barn and climbed into the loft. Good thing he'd replaced his phone with a throwaway. He didn't want any of his family overhear the conversation with his lawyer. Sinking onto an ancient straw bale, he leaned back against the wall and crossed his ankles.

"Drew, I just got off the phone with Abbie's attorney. What did you do to piss her off? She's hired a shark, and she's out for blood." The voice of his friend did nothing to calm his nerves.

"I didn't do anything. That's her natural temperament. She looks like an angel, but her motto is, *Take no prisoners.*" Drew sighed. "How much does she want?"

"Only everything, and she wants the divorce finalized by the first of October."

"That's next week! She wants everything I own and now she's telling me to hurry up?"

The lawyer's chuckle ramped Drew's heart rate into the stratosphere. "It seems she's got a wedding to go to in a month. Hers."

"I suspected something was going on between her and the new producer. She won't even have to pay the man." Puffs of dust rose in the still air as he paced the four steps across the loft and back again. He was at a loss for words. He shouldn't have been surprised, but he didn't think even Abbie was this callous. "Wait! She wants everything we own?"

"In the divorce decree she's claiming spousal abuse. She wants all the money—says she's earned it. The Porsche was mentioned along with any jewelry you've given her. And, she wants your third of the ranch."

Hearing Abbie's unreasonable demands, Drew dropped onto the straw bale again. The ranch? She couldn't—no wouldn't get her hands on his family's ranch. He must have been silent for too long because Mike was calling his name.

"Drew don't panic. This is their first volley." Mike's voice faded as he talked to someone in his office. "She's threatened to go to the press if she doesn't get what she wants. That's perfect."

"What do you mean, perfect. I don't want my name dragged through the mud." Drew absently climbed down the ladder and walked out of the barn. He focused his attention on the bluff where Dex and Mavis had built their house. The logs blended into the scenery like the structure had always been there.

"It's perfect because you don't have much to lose, and she has everything. The public won't want to see America's sweetheart embroiled in a nasty divorce. The tabloids will have a field day."

"Hell, I don't want to be fodder for the tabloids either." Drew placed his elbow against the corral post and dropped his head to rest on the top rail. "I'm still trying to wrap my head around the fact that she's trying to take everything I've worked for."

"I have one question. Abbie says she put money into the ranch to keep it going when your dad was ill. Did she?"

Drew heard the flick of a lighter, the intake of breath, and a long slow exhale. "I gave Dex what I could spare from my paycheck, small as it was. Abbie wasn't happy. She said we needed to save, but it's my ranch, too. I couldn't leave Dex to handle things alone."

"Try to take it easy, and I'll get back to you as soon as I have more news. Trust me, Drew. I know what I'm doing."

The line went dead. Drew stuffed his phone back into his pocket and turned to find Dex standing in the doorway.

"Problems?"

Drew glanced at his brother then back to the desert. "For me. Obviously not for Abbie." The day was warm, the wind was mild, and the birds sang. A cottontail rabbit hopped from one sagebrush to the next before disappearing down a hole. If he hadn't been married to a narcissistic woman, this day would be darn near perfect. Top it off with Dex hearing part of his conversation with the lawyer. No way would his brother walk away without knowing the truth. "Abbie's divorcing me."

Dex walked over to the fence and mimicked Drew's stance. "When did this start?"

"A few days ago. She called to tell me she'd already filed." Even after several days, the words didn't seem true. He kept waiting to wake up and find this was all a terrible dream. "She wants everything plus the ranch."

"She can't have it." Dex's features hardened into the determined man he'd become.

"I'm sorry, Dex. I've got my lawyer on it, but I'm worried. Abbie isn't above using anything to get what she wants. She's already planning her next wedding, and she only told me last week she wanted out of our marriage."

In a surprising move, Dex grinned, threw his arm

around Drew's shoulder, and moved him toward his house. "Come on, little brother. Let's go plan our revenge."

As they walked up the hill, Dex slugged Drew in the shoulder.

"Ow! What was that for?" Drew sidestepped out of reach.

"How long were you going to keep this divorce thing a secret? Didn't you think we'd figure it out eventually when Abbie didn't show up here anymore?"

"Let's face it. She's only been here twice in the six years we were married. It would have taken you a while to notice." Drew stepped through the back door and smiled at Mavis.

"Hey, Drew. You're in time for lunch. Make him a sandwich will you Dex? I'm late." Mavis grabbed her straw cowboy hat and picked up a bridle from a hook on the back door. She slung a small leather purse over her shoulder and reached for the doorknob.

Dex intercepted her, wrapping his arm around her waist. "We've got some good news, or not so good, depending on how you look at it."

"Let her go, Dex. She said she was late. We can discuss this later." Drew pulled a bottle of beer from the fridge and settled onto a bar stool by the counter. "It's not important, really."

Mavis froze and turned her attention to her husband. "I just remembered. I'm early. Now what's going on?" She settled on a stool next to Drew and rested her chin in her hand. "I'm all ears."

Drew sighed. If he knew one thing about his sister-in-law, it was that she was single-minded. "Abbie wants a divorce. In the next couple of weeks. So, she can marry her wealthy producer. That's the whole story." Tipping the icy Coors, he let several swallows flow down his throat. He hadn't been drunk for years, never had liked to drink a lot. Reaching out with his thumb, he swiped at the water drop snaking its way down the side of the bottle. Now he was wondering how many cold beers it would take to do the job.

"Oh, Drew. I'm so sorry." Mavis gave him a quick hug. "Unless you want this. Do you?"

He needed another couple of swallows to keep going. "You know Abbie. Nothing is ever easy with her."

"Do you want the divorce?" Leaning a little closer, Mavis placed her hand on his forearm.

"Yes, I do. Things haven't been right with us for quite a while."

"You said she wants everything." Dex sat beside him. "Which means what? She wants all your money?"

Drew nodded. Might as well get the whole story out. "She wants everything we have together plus my part of the ranch."

Silence filled the kitchen. Dex stood and moved over beside Mavis. They were both frozen in shock. Dex regained his voice first. "She can't have the ranch. If I have to burn it to the ground, she won't get her hands on the Rafter D."

The hug Mavis gave Drew this time wasn't quick. He could feel the tremors shaking her body. "We'll fight her."

Drew pulled in a breath. "I want you to buy me out."

"No!" Dex's voice was sharp and final. "No."

"Abbie is about to sign a huge record deal. She'll bankrupt us out of spite." Drew poured the rest of the beer down the drain. He'd suddenly lost his appetite for alcohol. Turning to his family, he shook his head. "If I don't own the ranch, she can't get her hands on it. It's the only way I can think of to keep the Rafter D safe."

Mavis took each of their arms and led them to the kitchen chairs. She took the seat between them. "Have you asked your lawyer about this? Will it keep the ranch safe or will she be able to prove you sold to keep it from her?"

"He's supposed to call me back in a couple of days. He said he needed time to talk to her attorney. The attorney who is being paid by my not quite ex-wife's producer. Another reason for me to sell you the ranch." How the hell did he get himself into this fix? He snorted. He got into this mess by believing Abbie was as honest as the rest of his family. He'd been a sucker from their first date.

Dex laid his hand on Drew's shoulder. "We'll figure a way out of this. The first thing we need to know is if selling your portion to us will keep the ranch safe. Talk to your attorney as soon as you can. Mavis and I can move some money around and take out a loan if that's what it takes."

The back door opened to let in a breeze. Davie stepped back and ushered Randi inside. "How come we weren't invited to the party? Don't you guys like us anymore?"

Randi grinned up at her husband then shifted her gaze to Mavis. "You're late. I'm all saddled and ready to go."

Rafe followed them in. "You must have forgotten my invitation, too."

Davie settled into a chair, and Randi plopped onto his lap. "What's up?"

Mavis stood and pulled Randi to her feet. "Drew and Dex can tell you two what's going on, and I'll fill Randi in on the way to the barrel race."

As she and Randi gave their husbands a kiss before leaving, Drew got a sharp pain where his heart used to be. Not that he missed Abbie, but he longed for the love his brothers had found. Looking back, the only reason he and Abbie had been a team was because he was doing what she wanted. If he'd insisted they live on the ranch, she'd have left him years ago.

Davie's curse brought Drew's attention back to his brothers and Rafe. "We need to put our heads together and come up with a plan. Maybe we could kidnap that witch and hold her in a tent on the range until she cracks. Abbie wouldn't last a day without her blow dryer and her phone. She'd give up any rights to the ranch and anything else Drew wants." He tipped the kitchen chair he sat in back on its legs and grinned.

"Or we could put her in Dex's basement and force her to listen to elevator music until she agrees to be kind." Rafe grinned as he got his own beer.

Leave it to Rafe to come up with a not-evil solution. "Good plan, but Dex doesn't have a basement." As bad as his life had become, Drew couldn't stop his laugh. Leave it to Davie and Rafe to find something funny in the unholy mess his life had become. "And Davie, you might be right, but we'd have to get our hands on her first. My attorney told me Abbie has decided she needs round the clock protection. The woman is absolutely paranoid."

"She's not paranoid if I decide to go after her." Dex's voice came out as a growl. "Call your lawyer now and find out if a sale to us would protect the ranch."

Drew walked into the living room as he dialed the number. After a quick conversation, he thanked Michael.

Dex still sat at the table, but Davie had his head in the refrigerator. "Want something to eat? Mavis isn't much of a cook, but there's cold pizza in here."

Dex grinned. "Davie's right about Mavis' cooking, but she has other qualities that make up for her less-than-perfect culinary skills.

"I got through to Michael. Here's the quick version. I might get away with selling my part of the ranch to you, but that might backfire. The problem is she's claiming she gave money to keep the ranch going. He did say if I could sell to someone not in the family and had a reason for doing so, it might hold up in court." Drew took the slice of pizza Davie handed to him then pulled a paper towel off the rack. He slid into one of the chairs and took a bite.

"Who would that be?" Davie asked.

Drew shrugged. "As my first and second picks are part of the family, Rafe is the logical choice."

Rafe swallowed his bite of pizza, his expression forlorn. "You all know owning part of the ranch would be my dream come true, but I don't have that kind of money, and this needs to be above board."

***

Gina walked around the flatbed trailer for the third time, checking the load. As the owner of Homedale Hotshots Custom Trucking, she was so busy she couldn't tell day from night. At least the weather was on her side for once.

She pulled a rag from her back pocket and wiped at a smudge of grease from the fender of her dark blue one-ton Dodge. As a one-woman show, she hauled anything that would fit on her 24-foot flatbed, as long as it wasn't illegal, immoral, or just plain icky.

When her godfather, Howard Tiner, had died suddenly a few years ago, she'd pulled in a deep breath, taken out a loan with Gladys as her co-signer, and stepped into a business partnership with her godmother. The Tiners had been the one stable part of her childhood. When she'd become pregnant, they were the only ones to offer to help. She hadn't told any of the other townspeople. Embarrassment had sealed her mouth.

Gladys had arranged for Gina and her mother to live with Gladys' sister until after the baby was born. They'd spread the story around town that Gina's mother had found a job in Florida.

Howard had helped Gina arrange the adoption then offered her a job when she'd graduated high school.

When Howard had died suddenly, the kind women had helped her learn the business and coached her until she knew the ropes.

When Gladys decided to move to Florida, Gina had refinanced and taken on all the responsibilities that came along with being the sole owner. Not that she minded. Shortly after graduating high school, she'd realized if she wanted anything out of life, it was up to her to go get it.

Gina grasped the tie downs on her trailer and pulled,

testing the tightness. Dropping the load of irrigation pipe onto the freeway when she delivered it tomorrow wasn't the way to get more customers.

Now, if she could get the frantic ramblings of her mind to shut off. Anxiety had been her constant companion lately, along with insomnia. Falling asleep at the wheel was another thing that wasn't going to happen. She leaned against the truck and took several deep breaths, relaxing her muscles.

As she watched, the sun faded to orange and pink streaks in the evening sky. She hadn't taken the time to eat since breakfast, and a burger and fries would go a long way toward making her feel human again. One of these days she was going to have to do something about her diet, but with the frantic pace of her life, that item was far down on the list.

She hopped into the rattletrap '79 Ford Ranchero she kept for running around her small hometown. Another item way down the list was restoring this baby. She patted the dash and turned the key.

Benny's Burgers was the best place for fast food. It was also the only place. She'd finished her burger and was dragging the last of her fries through a cup of special sauce when the passenger door opened, and Drew slid into the seat.

He opened the bag he held and pulled out a double cheeseburger, a large order of fries, and another one of tater tots. After swallowing his first bite of the sandwich, he grinned. "So, we meet again, Wally."

"I asked you not to call me that." Gina wadded up her wrappers along with the bag. Her heart sped up at the sight of the middle Dunbar brother, and she hammered the useless emotion back down where it belonged. Life was only tolerable when she traveled through it alone. "What do you want?"

Drew took another big bite, waving his hand to tell her to wait for his answer. He finally swallowed and grinned.

"I saw you sitting here alone, and I was alone, so I thought we could eat dinner alone together."

"Really?" Her brows drew down into a frown. This man wanted something, and she didn't have anything to give. "After all these years you choose now to decide to have dinner with me. When did we become such good friends?"

Drew lowered his burger and turned to face her. "We've always been friends."

"No, we were raised around each other. Your brothers and my friends were friends, but I wouldn't call you and I buddies. Face it. You haven't taken a second look at me since that kiss my sophomore year in high school. You must not have been impressed."

"That's not true. I've always liked you."

"Come on. You haven't thought of me in years. Now, you're all alone. Now, you need someone to hang out with." If the state of her life hadn't been so sad, she'd have found this funny.

Drew looked confused. He rewrapped the burger and put the potatoes back into the bag. "I—." He cleared his throat but kept his gaze on the burger bag. "There's probably some truth in that."

"I have enough trouble taking care of myself, I don't have time to babysit you." A wave of guilt swept over her at his expression. Fatigue and worry were causing her to take out her frustrations on Drew. She ran her fingers through her hair. "I didn't mean that. I'm not sleeping well, and I have several jobs back to back. I'll be on the road for nearly twenty hours tomorrow."

"I heard you bought the Homedale Hotshots. Don't you have any back up drivers?"

"I can barely scrape enough together to pay my bills. No way could I afford to hire someone else." A small smile played across her lips. The hardships were worth it to be her own boss. "The joys of owning my own business."

Drew clutched the food bag in one hand and opened the door. "I won't waste anymore of your time." He climbed out and shut the car door with a quiet click. But before she could react, he opened it again.

"Back so soon?" Gina gave him a real smile this time. It was true, they hadn't been close, but Drew had always been nice to her when others hadn't.

He settled into the seat, leaving one booted foot on the pavement. "Hear me out before you say no."

"What do you want, and what makes you think I'll say no?"

"I know that much about you. You'd refuse to take anyone's help unless you were desperate. I'm not offering to help. I'm offering a trade."

Drew wasn't usually cryptic. He'd piqued her interest for sure. She raised her eyebrows and waited for him to continue.

"I've got a big problem." Drew pulled his foot in and closed the car door.

"Don't we all? What makes yours so much bigger than everyone else's?"

Drew tipped his head against the headrest and sighed. "Not a huge problem in the overall scheme of things, but for my brothers and I, it could be catastrophic. I might lose my part of the ranch."

Gina sat upright and placed her palm on Drew's shoulder. "I shouldn't have made fun of you. That would be awful. If I had any money, I'd loan you some to help with your payments."

"Thanks, but I don't owe money. That's the one thing Abbie wanted that I wouldn't do. No, the lovely Abbie Anjelica, America's Sweetheart, wants everything I own as part of our divorce settlement." Drew massaged his forehead with his fingertips. "I'd give her anything else, but I can't let her have the ranch. Not my dad's ranch."

Gina nodded before climbing out of the car. She walked to the trashcan to give him time to corral his emotions.

The three brothers had been different from childhood. Dex had been focused on rodeo.

Davie had been the local wild child.

Drew was the steadfast one, reliable and genuine. The one who'd worn his emotions on his sleeve.

After a few minutes, she returned to the car, bent down, and peered through the window into driver's side. "What can I do to help? I could borrow a backhoe and dig a grave if you want. I wouldn't even charge you." She'd hoped to get a smile, but Drew continued to stare out the windshield. She waited a second before sliding back into the car.

At the sound of the engine starting, Drew looked up.

"I've got an idea. Want to go with me?" In the few minutes it took for Drew to nod, Gina had pulled out of the parking lot and driven to the only convenience store. "Wait here." She hurried inside and bought a six-pack of Corona.

As she came out the door, she saw Drew leaning against the front fender, his legs crossed at the ankles.

"What are you up to? What's in the bag?"

Gina couldn't stop her smile this time. "I know what you need to cheer you up. Get in." She placed the bag in the bed of the small truck and slid into the driver's seat.

It took fifteen minutes more or less to get to the destination Gina had in mind. When she turned off the ignition, except for the songbirds, the area was quiet. Pulling a blanket from behind the seat, she lowered the tailgate, and climbed into the back. "Best view in the valley."

Drew leaned with his elbows on the fender, his chin in his hands. He watched her spread the blanket. "I haven't been out here since high school. We had some wild parties, didn't we?"

Gina just nodded. At all the high school parties she'd attended, she'd felt like an outsider. Everyone else seemed to find it easy to pair up. The one time she'd thought she'd found the right boy he'd only been interested in one thing. She'd learned that lesson the hard way when the baby had come. Taking a deep breath, she cleared her mind before twisting the top of a beer.

The desert smelled of sage and sunshine, two of her favorite scents. The grayish green of the sagebrush rolled across the low hills toward the canyons of the Owyhee River. A Goshen hawk soared on the warm air currents.

Drew stood beside her and stared out at the landscape. "It sounds so cliché, but life seemed so simple then. I never wanted to leave the ranch. My plans were to help my dad and brothers, get married, and have a couple of boys to carry on the tradition." He leaped into the back of the Ranchero with the grace of a dancer then turned his head, so their eyes met.

Gina crossed her eyes and stuck her tongue out at him. "What! Girls can't ranch?" When he smiled, she reached into the bag and handed him a beer. Fishing in her pocket, she came up with a small pocketknife.

"Okay, okay, don't stab me. I wouldn't have minded a girl." He lifted the bottle to his mouth.

"You dork! Can't have a Corona without a lime." She cut a slice of the lime she'd bought along with the beer and handed it to him. As they sipped and took in the scenery, she didn't feel the need for conversation.

Apparently, neither did he.

The sun sank below the horizon, leaving an electric colored sky in its wake. Perfect for enjoying a couple of good beers with good company. When the area was fully dark, Drew spoke.

"Thanks."

"No problem. Sometimes a person needs to get away." She took in the stars and the sliver of moon. "I've spent many an evening here trying to figure out my life."

"You brought me to your private getaway?" Drew swallowed the last of his beer and pulled another out of the bag.

"I'm not sure it's a very good spot. I don't seem to be able to figure out anything." And that was the truth.

He shifted his weight and ran his hand down the side of the truck bed. "When did you get this? It's a beauty."

She looked at the scuffed olive-green paint. The Ranchero had seen better days, but so had she. "I don't know. It needs a lot of work."

"Nothing wrong with work. This is a classic. Are you going to fix it up?" Drew hopped out of the truck bed and walked to the front. "What's under the hood?"

Gina had forgotten Drew's love of cars. That and their love of animals had been the only things they'd had in common. Before she could get out of the back, Drew had popped the hood.

"Holy shit! You've got a 352 V8 with a four-barrel Holley carburetor in this puppy. With custom headers!"

Pleasure that someone else saw the potential in the little truck spread a smile across her face. She clinked her bottle against his. "Yup, with custom headers."

CHAPTER THREE

Drew sipped the strong-enough-to-eat-paint coffee Nana Lucy made each morning as he drove the old ranch truck toward Homedale. The evening spent with Gina had been a comfortable and sorely needed interlude from his problems, but when he woke in the morning, his troubles were as big as ever.

Before he'd even cleared the driveway, the smell of diesel exhaust filled the cab. The weather had cooled, but he needed fresh air. The window crank handle made half a circle before falling off in his hand. With fumes this thick, by the time he made it to town, he'd be high as a kite.

Even as he worked not to, his thoughts turned back to Abbie. Michael had called several more times, but still hadn't found a foolproof way to keep the ranch safe from his ex-wife's grasping hands.

The Dunbar brothers couldn't take even a small chance of letting her get any kind of control.

Sunday morning traffic in Homedale was non-existent. Just like the Monday through Saturday traffic. The only time too many vehicles became a problem were the fall and winter evenings when the local high school football or basketball teams had home games.

The night before he'd wanted to offer to help Gina drive today, but he'd become sidetracked when they'd started talking about Abbie and the ranch. The thought of his almost-ex having control of even a part of the Rafter D made his skin crawl. As vindictive as she'd become, she'd sell her part to some dude who'd want to raise llamas.

Pulling into Gina's driveway, he spotted her walking around the trailer loaded with twelve-inch irrigation pipe.

She glanced up and did a double take. "What are you doing here this early?"

He leaned against the truck fender and studied her. Something was different. The early morning sun made her tanned skin glow, and she pushed a blonde lock behind her ear.

Her hair! Drew didn't think he'd ever seen Gina's hair down. Even in middle school, it had always been in a thick braid down her back. The loose strands fell in waves around her face.

He took a step closer and nearly reached out to touch the curls.

Gina took a step back and glared.

She hadn't been thrilled to see him when he'd arrived. He could imagine what she'd do if he ran his fingers through her hair.

Crossing her arms, she waited for him to answer, and he grinned wider at the sight of her impatience. "I got to thinking. I'm sitting at the ranch without much to do. Dex and Davie work like a well-oiled machine." His smile faltered at the thought that his brothers didn't need him.

"Abbie didn't only ruin your marriage. She stole your job." Gina's face held traces of pity.

Pity was one thing Drew didn't need. "I think I have an idea. You need help. I need a job. We're perfect for each other."

Gina turned on her heel and strode toward the house.

Drew straightened. It was obvious he didn't understand women, and this one took the cake. Unsure if she'd let him enter if he knocked, he walked in like he owned the place.

She stood, her back to him, staring out the kitchen window at the pasture next door.

He watched her for a moment, going over their conversation, trying to figure out what he'd said that was wrong. "Did I say something to make you mad?"

She whirled, her jaw set. "I heard you say you needed a job. I need the help. The only problem is I can't afford to pay you."

"That is a problem. Let me see. First off, I owe you for hauling my car to town."

"I did that as a friend. You know that." She crossed her arms and glared as if daring him to contradict her.

Well, let the games begin. "Last night, you said we weren't friends. So, I owe you, and I don't like being in debt any more than you do."

"Okay then, that little amount won't buy me much of your time."

"Then, how about you trade hauling things to the ranch for my wages. That way I'll have a way to help Dex and Davie, and you'll have a backup driver."

Her face softened, and she almost smiled before she caught herself. Narrowing her eyes, she glared at him. "You've got a deal under one condition." She grabbed a worn brown vest and threaded an arm through the sleeve hole. "I'm the only boss."

Drew followed her as she strode out to the truck. "I can live with that." He climbed into the passenger seat. "For now." He kept the last words low enough that she couldn't hear. No use getting her all riled up before they even left the driveway.

"I heard you, and if you want to work for me, you'll do as I say."

He thought he saw a grin on her pretty lips, but when she fully faced him, her expression was no-nonsense in a way that only Gina could do. "Hey, boss lady. Whatever you say goes. Even if you're wrong."

"One question I forgot to ask." Gina climbed into the truck and turned the key before looking at him again. "You do know how to pull a trailer this long, don't you?"

Again, he saw a hint of a smile and decided to have some fun. "Well, Abbie and I had a little camp trailer when we first went on the road, so I have some experience hauling." He put a bit of exasperation into his voice. "I only backed it into something a couple of times. Maybe you're right. I'll just be your co-pilot and read the map."

Gina hit the brakes. "Now, I know you're making fun of me."

"What makes you say that?" She didn't seem to be able to keep the amusement from her expression.

"Well, mainly because the GPS is right in front of you. Do people really use maps anymore?" She pulled out onto the road and headed down the county lane toward the freeway. "I'll drive until I get tired then you can take over."

"Where are we going?" Drew tipped the seat back a little and settled in for the drive. He really didn't care where they were going as long as he didn't have to sit at the ranch and see his brothers' pitying looks. Even worse was the mothering his grandmother and sisters-in-law insisted on lavishing on him.

"We're taking part of these pipes to Idaho Falls and the rest along with the generator are going to Ogden. I've got a load coming back from Ogden to Boise, so I'll get paid both ways."

***

The feel of the truck wallowing through road construction woke Drew. They were halfway to their first customer. "Sorry about that. I've really made a great impression on you, taking a nap the first half hour on the job."

"That's okay. If you're going to sleep, its best to do it while I'm driving. Just don't nod off when you're at the wheel." She reached out and turned the radio station down. "Mind if I ask you a question?"

Drew thought for a moment. Although he was positive the question would be about Abbie, he found he didn't mind. "Go ahead if I can reserve the right not to answer."

She nodded and seemed to be gathering her thoughts before she spoke. "What did you ever see in Abigail?"

"That might take some time. Right now, I'm not sure." Drew dropped his feet from the dash and tilted the seat upright. "I certainly didn't see the real Abbie. I think she loved me at the beginning, but she has stars in her eyes. I don't have much to give to that goal anymore."

"You know, even when I thought their marriages weren't the right thing to do, I could see what Dex and Davie saw in their wives. But Abbie? Nope, never saw the attraction."

Drew pulled a bottle of water from the small cooler he'd brought along. After taking a long draw, he turned to her. "What didn't you like about her?"

Gina screwed up her face as if the answer were painful. "You'll laugh."

"Probably but tell me anyway."

"She never looked at you with love in her eyes." Gina fixed her gaze on the road and didn't say anything else.

They slowed as traffic made its way around a car with a flat on the side of the road. Gina handled the loaded truck and trailer with ease, and Drew gained a little more respect for this quiet woman.

"Go on."

"Well, if you watch Mavis and Dex or Davie and Randi, those women can't keep their eyes of their men." She snorted, and Drew had to laugh. "Hell, most of the time, they can't keep their hands off of them."

Drew had to agree. He'd noticed that through the years. Abbie never was touchy feely, but he'd chalked it up to her being shy. Now that he thought about it, he realized how much he'd rationalized. Abbie wasn't shy at all. She simply hadn't cared enough.

"Look, Drew. I'm sorry. I should learn to keep my big mouth shut." She downshifted when traffic became heavier as they neared Pocatello.

"You've got nothing to be sorry about. You were telling the truth."

"Yeah, but it's none of my business. Most people fall in love with an inappropriate person sometime in their lives. You happened to marry yours." Her eyes widened, and she focused her attention out the window. "Luckily, I didn't get that choice, or I'd have made the same mistake."

Drew's snort caused her gaze to snap to him. In an attempt to stop his laughter, he cleared his throat. It didn't work. "I married my mistake? Right to the point as usual. I did have some second thoughts during the days before the wedding when Abbie didn't have one opinion on how or where we should get married. I figured lots of people have cold feet."

"Should have listened to your feet." Gina's smile widened, and her shoulders relaxed. "Look, it's not like I'm an expert at relationships. I can't even find a boyfriend. I just think you can do better than self-centered Abigail."

They drove in silence for a while. Drew let his thoughts wander, thinking over what Gina had said. His brothers had told him the same thing over the years, but they'd always flavored the advice with pity and sarcasm. Why hadn't he paid attention before this? "I'm going to have to keep you around to check out my decisions from now on."

"No!"

He'd meant it as a joke, but apparently Gina didn't think it was funny.

"I spent a long time trying to convince your brothers I knew more about the women they loved than they did. Fortunately, they ignored me. You're on your own now. I'm done in the advice for the lovelorn department."

***

Gina fitted the nozzle into the gas tank then looked up to see Drew striding toward the truck stop store. It had been years since she'd seen him in a pair of Wranglers, and to say that was a crime was an understatement. This man did more for the denim jeans than either of his brothers.

In her perfect world, it would be against the law for a hot man to wear khakis. She gripped the nozzle tighter as she watched him walk across the pavement. No matter how hard she'd tried, a perfect world seemed to evade all her efforts.

She was still staring, lost in her thoughts, as Drew came out of the store. When their eyes met, his eyebrows raised. "Something wrong?"

She shook her head, her cheeks warming. How long had it been since she'd blushed? She hesitated, sure she was going to put her foot in her mouth again, but years ago, she'd promised herself she'd always tell the truth no matter the cost. Her little white lies had been the devil's playground. "Just admiring your Wranglers."

"Some people would call that objectification." A smile spread across Drew's face. "Me? I'd like to say thank you."

"Don't tell me Abbie didn't like Wranglers. She's a country western star." She folded the receipt and slid it into her wallet before climbing into the driver's seat.

Drew leaned into the open passenger door and settled two giant soft drink cups into the holders. He glanced up and caught her eye. "She loved Wranglers and cowboy hats and boots. She just didn't love them on me. As her manager, I was supposed to be unobtrusive, stay in the background, hide from the spotlight, that sort of thing."

Gina studied his dark eyes, black hair, and muscles. Oh, those muscles. This man couldn't be inconspicuous in his sleep—or in a coma. "In other words, she wanted all the attention."

"In other words, you're exactly right." Drew climbed

into the truck and pointed to one of the drinks. "Are you still a soda hater?"

She leveled a look on him then relaxed. He wanted to change the subject, and that was fine with her. "I still don't drink sugar. However, unless you've changed, you'll drink both of those with ease."

Drew waggled the large cup and grinned. "Try this. I think you'll like it."

Gina peered in the top and tried to see what was inside. Taking a sip, she smiled. "Iced tea. No matter what everyone else says about you, you are a good man."

"I've been trying to tell people that, but no one seems to believe me." He stopped and looked at her. "Do you want me to drive for a while? I'm a good driver, too."

It was a tempting offer, but Gina wasn't ready to turn over her rig yet. If Drew hadn't shown up, she'd be making this trip by herself. She'd done it before, and she'd be doing it again. "I've got it."

By the time they'd unloaded the pipes in Idaho Falls, it was near noon. They grabbed burgers and headed for Ogden. Once they'd delivered to her second customer, she drove across town and picked up the load she'd contracted to take back to Boise.

She'd decided to drive the entire trip. As owner of the Homedale Hotshots, she didn't need any help. A yawn slipped out, and she glanced at Drew to see if he'd caught it.

He was engrossed in a music industry magazine he must have gotten at the truck stop.

Another yawn nearly took control. The long hours and the lack of sleep the night before had caught up. "Talk to me, Drew. Tell me some more stories about being on the road with the world's sweetest country ingénue."

Drew turned down the radio and reclined his seat. Pulling his cap over his eyes, he sighed. "Let's see. Do you want to know about the time she left me in Dallas, or the time she disappeared for two days then told me she'd gone to a spa for a break?"

"And you didn't have a clue? Come on, Drew. I've wondered about your judgment from time to time, but I never thought you were stupid." She flipped on her blinker and passed a semi crawling onto the freeway. Realizing she'd heaped an insult on top of his confession, she considered apologizing. Only one word came out. "Sorry." The word seemed inadequate, but a woman who'd promised herself to be brutally honest in everything, it was all she had.

Drew gave her a contrite smile. "I went through life assuming I was pretty smart. I'm rethinking that belief. No wonder you won't let me drive. You probably think I'll wreck your truck."

She glanced away from the road to see if he was joking. He was staring out the side window at the small town they were passing as if it were the Emerald City. The tense silence smothered any further conversation, and Gina focused on the road. The things Drew had told her played over and over in her mind.

Abigail Beaker had been a royal pain in the ass since the first time she'd set foot in Homedale at the age of fourteen. Drew had been enamored with the skinny blonde from the start. She'd been tiny and fair and cute as a bug.

Everything Gina wasn't.

Abbie also had a secret nasty streak she'd only shown to those she thought couldn't further her career. Although Gina hadn't been impressed with the woman's vocal talents, the rest of the world was. The young singer had shot to the top of the charts with her first single.

There was no accounting for taste.

Drew leaned back and pulled his cap over his eyes without another word.

One of these days she was going to learn to self-censor before her thoughts exploded out of her mouth. She'd enjoyed the trip until she'd hurt Drew's feelings, and that was something she hadn't meant to do.

Her eyes drifted closed, and she shook her head to ward off the sleepies. Only three hours to go. She could do this. Hitting the window button, she let chilly air into the cab.

Drew sat up, rubbing his eyes. He glanced at her for a long moment, and she thought he might go back to sleep. Instead, he took several swallows of the now flat soda and grinned. "Better let me drive—or else."

She stiffened. "Or else?" Her question came out with a hard edge. "Or else what?"

He did a slow stretch that showed off his toned abs and hard muscles. "One of two things will happen." When she just watched the road, he continued. "One, you drift off to sleep and wreck your truck, injuring both of us. Or, two, you pull over and take a nap, wasting time while I sit here and twiddle my thumbs. Neither is an efficient way to run your business."

Gina would have liked to be insulted. Her only problem was that he was right. Most trips she could do the driving of herself, but this time she needed to show a little gratitude. Drew would take care of her truck and her business. If she was sure of anything, it was that. She stifled a smile. No way was she giving up without a fight. "You have a current CDL license, right?"

He nodded and smiled. "Before Abbie really hit the big time, I drove the band's motorhome."

"No outstanding tickets? No wrecks?" She struggled to maintain her no-nonsense expression. She knew from experience, if she gave any of the Dunbar brothers the slightest bit of slack, they'd take over. Pulling off on the next exit, she decided to give up control for the time being.

Gina held in her sigh of relief as she watched the headlights on the other side of the freeway slide past. Ten years ago, there wouldn't have been half this much traffic at this hour of the night, but you couldn't stop progress.

Relaxing her stiff shoulder muscles, she tipped her head

back against the headrest. Within a few miles, her fatigue would have forced her to let Drew drive. This way she hadn't appeared to give in.

Just as she closed her eyes, she realized what he'd done.

In his quiet Drew way, he hadn't forced the issue. He'd left the choice up to her. He'd allowed her to save face.

Something very few people in her life had done.

STEPHANIE BERGET

CHAPTER FOUR

Drew pulled the brim of his cap lower to block the sun as he hurried across the parking lot. The day was bright, but November had arrived along with Old Man Winter. With the wind dropping the temperature into the teens, Drew hurried up the shrub-lined walkway of Boise's largest hospital.

He strode through the double electronic doors then made his way toward the emergency room. It had been a little over three weeks since he'd accompanied Gina on the trip, and she hadn't asked him to help again.

When she'd called at ten-fifteen as he was moving heifers from one pasture to another, he'd been surprised. It was a stroke of luck he'd been in the one spot where he could pick up cell service.

She'd been closed-mouthed about the extent of her injuries, just asked him to come to the hospital, and he wasn't sure what to expect as he entered the room. Lying in the bed, her skin was nearly as white as the sheets, her arm in a sling. A large bruise darkened the flesh around her right eye.

He tiptoed in and carefully moved to the chair closer to the bed.

"I'm awake. You don't have to sneak around." She didn't open her eyes, and her words were slightly slurred.

"How ya doing, Crash?" Pretty sure he shouldn't show sympathy for this strong woman, he went with humor instead. "You'll get your deliveries done faster if you don't get into a battle with a semi at eighty miles an hour."

"He had it coming. He was taking up more than his half of the pavement."

He thought she might have tried to laugh, but the sound was so faint he couldn't be sure it wasn't a groan. "So how long before you can blow this pop-stand?"

She struggled to sit straighter. "Better be soon. I have a load scheduled for this afternoon."

"What did the doctor have to say?" Drew leaned back in his chair and crossed one ankle over the other knee. "Or are we not allowed to acknowledge the fact that you're hurt?"

"No secret. My collarbone's broke."

"And?" He crossed his arms. Getting any personal information from this woman was tough, but he'd had lots of practice dealing with egotistical producers.

"And, what?" She turned her head and focused her attention on the room's only window.

He let the silence surround them and waited.

"Alright. I have a concussion—a small one. Hardly worth mentioning. A short nap and I'll be fine to drive."

Drew didn't even try to stop his laughter. So like Gina. Cantankerous and acerbic, so why did his mind keep replaying their conversations? Why did she keep invading his thoughts?

And, why was it was so hard for her to ask for help?

He knew he wouldn't be here if there was any way she could have driven herself home. He dropped his chin to his chest and feigned nonchalance. "How are you going to shift with only one arm?"

She'd opened her mouth to answer when a nurse entered the room. "I see your ride has arrived. Are you ready to get out of here?"

With a minimum of grumbling, most of which was about why it took so long to get out of a hospital, he'd gotten Gina released. When they'd made their way to the pickup, he opened the door. She looked so frail and exhausted he felt an overwhelming need to protect her. "Need some help getting in? This pickup is a long way off the ground."

She gave him a glare, but when she tried to lever herself into the truck with one arm, he saw her wobble. Wrapping one arm around her shoulder, he slipped the other one beneath her thighs and lifted her onto the seat. With a grin, he slammed the door.

He climbed into the driver's seat and glanced at Gina. "You can thank me later."

Her head rested against the seatback and her eyes were closed. Her voice was so soft, he almost missed the words. "Thanks, Drew, for everything."

"No problem. That's what white knights are for." He'd hoped to get a laugh, but she merely sighed.

As they left the congestion of Boise behind, Drew glanced at her. She'd leaned the seat back and closed her eyes. "You said you have a delivery today. Only one?"

She nodded, grimaced, and a low groan escaped. "I sure don't need this headache."

"Concussions will do that to you."

"Yes, good thing the delivery today isn't very far. Tucker's up at Rye Valley need a load of roofing shingles. I'm pretty sure I can borrow a truck and trailer from Mike's Auto. Well, I can rent one. Mike doesn't give anything away for free." When he only gave her a skeptical glance, she continued. "This couldn't have come at a worse time. I've got deliveries every day next week, and my payment to Gladys is due."

"I'm sure Gladys will give you more time if you explain what happened." Drew shifted down as they came to the off-ramp for Homedale. After maneuvering through the outskirts of Caldwell, they were on the country road leading home. "She's always been an understanding woman."

Gina snorted then groaned. She reached up and softly touched her collarbone before speaking. "Yes, she is. She's the best, but I don't do business that way. I owe her, and I'll pay on time if I have to carry the loads on my back."

Drew didn't contradict her. He knew if pushed, she might try to do that very thing. Pulling into her driveway, he helped her into the house. When he had her settled onto the couch, he sank into the overstuffed chair. "Why don't you let me take over for you today? Then we'll figure out the rest."

Gina struggled to her feet with a groan before plopping back onto the couch. She couldn't even stand without getting dizzy.

Drew just watched. No matter how badly she wanted to avoid asking for help, he knew she wouldn't endanger others if she wasn't fit to drive.

"Okay, for today only. The address is on my—"

"I know the Tucker Ranch. Dex and I high school rodeoed with Cane Tucker. What time were you supposed to be there?"

"Three. But I need to call Mike about the rig."

"Dex is already on his way with the ranch truck and trailer. And we don't charge a rental fee. Now you sit still while I find you something to eat." Drew made a peanut butter and orange marmalade sandwich with the last two slices of bread and poured the dregs from a bag of Fritos on the plate. "You don't stock much food, do you?"

She ignored his dig, as her eyes focused on his face. "I'll pay you for the use of your truck. I don't take charity."

He stopped and stared at her. This woman was stubborn as a mule on a hundred-degree day. "This isn't charity, Wally. Its help from your neighbors."

As she shifted, a grimace of pain crossed her face

before she pulled on her normal no-nonsense attitude. "If it's all the same to you, I'd rather pay."

"Suit yourself, but I've got to warn you, Dex thinks pretty highly of his old truck." Drew grabbed the quilt folded on the back of the old rocker and spread it over her. He'd seen the shiver she tried to hide. "I'm not sure you should be left alone."

The derisive snort sounded more like the old Gina. "I've been taking care of myself since I was ten. I think I can lay on the couch until you get back without falling off."

Drew glanced around the room. The 70s oak coffee table was battered beyond repair. The floral upholstery on the matching sofa and recliner had faded to a lackluster tan, and one of the doors from the ancient china hutch in the corner sat on the floor, leaning against the wall. It looked like Gina had never bought a new piece of furniture in her adult life. He pulled the shabby coffee table closer to where she lay, testing it for strength before placing her lunch and a glass of water on it. "I'll take your delivery if you promise to stay put until I get back."

"I promise." Her answer had come too quickly, but she'd try to complete the order herself if he didn't leave.

He leaned over her and tucked the quilt around her body. "I'll be back soon."

"You're treating me like an infant."

"Just because I'm helping you doesn't mean I think of you as a child." Far from it. Drew hadn't meant to say his thoughts out loud, and the sound of tires on gravel gave him the excuse to leave before she told him again how she could take care of herself. "See you in about three hours."

By the time Drew got outside, his brother stood leaning against the fender of the 1992 one-ton Dodge. The blue paint was scratched, and the right front fender was crumpled. Bad as the truck looked, Drew knew from experience the old beast ran as good as it did the day it came off the showroom floor. "Thanks for bringing this down."

"No problem. How's Gina doing?"

"Broken collarbone and concussion. You got time to stay with her while I run this up to Rye Valley?"

"I'll do better than that. Mavis and Randi are on their way." Dex's grin couldn't have been wider. "There they are now. I'm out of here before Gina finds out."

"Coward!" Drew called after his brother as the man backed out of the driveway in Drew's truck. There was no love lost between Gina and his sisters-in-law, although the brothers hadn't been able to figure out what the problem was.

Mavis and Randi waved as they pulled past him. Climbing from the car, they filled their arms with grocery sacks and headed for the house.

He watched the door close behind the women then drove the rig out of the driveway without a backward glance. Time for him to make his getaway, too.

He'd called Dex a coward, but now he had to admit, he wasn't any braver than his brother when it came to these three women.

***

Gina closed her eyes and faked sleep as soon as she realized Drew had left Mavis and Randi to take care of her while he was gone. Leave it to the thoughtful Dunbar brother to ignore her when she said she could take care of herself.

The women had checked on her every few minutes. Fortunately, they'd spent most of the time at the kitchen table or they'd have driven her bat-shit crazy. She wasn't used to having people in her home. For years she'd chosen to keep to herself.

Maybe not the best plan.

The worst part was she could hear their quiet voices but couldn't make out the words. Probably talking about how she was trying to trap brother number three.

Logically, she knew that was paranoia talking.

She managed to lift herself into a sitting position then thought better of the move. Laying down, she closed her eyes and massaged her brows.

Mavis and Randi had always been kind. Her fingers balled into fists. One thing her mother had drilled into her head was that people couldn't be trusted. Being a loner was lonely, all right, but that way she didn't have to worry about someone stabbing her in the back.

"Are you awake?" The quiet voice startled her, and her eyes popped open.

Randi stood beside the couch, a look of concern on her face.

Just what Gina didn't need, a big dose of pity from the Good Luck sisters. "What are you doing here?" The three women had been friends until sometime during their junior year of high school. That was the year her life fell apart.

No matter what she attempted, the bad luck gnome slapped her with his stick, while these two women got everything she'd ever wanted.

Randi hadn't answered her question, and that made her even more uncomfortable. Drew was going to suffer when he got back. "I asked what you're doing in my house." As she attempted to sit up, a sharp jab reminded her of her injuries. As if she needed reminding. She fell back against the pillow and tried to phrase an apology.

"We brought food and a movie if you feel up to it," Mavis said.

Didn't that take the cake? They were hiding their pity behind kindness. "Look, I'm fine. I just need a nap. You can go home."

Randi glanced at Mavis then sat in the ladder back chair next to Gina. "We'll go."

Surprise coursed through Gina. Was that all it took? It couldn't be this easy to get rid of the women.

"Yes, we'll leave as soon as you tell us how to explain to the Dex, Davie, and Drew that we left you here to fend for yourself." Mavis stood at the end of the couch, her fingers tucked into the front pockets of her jeans, her expression as serious as a Pentecostal preacher on Sunday morning.

A smile almost escaped from Gina's lips. They had a point. "Tell them I ran you off with my shotgun. They'll believe that." She'd been known for her prowess with guns in high school. She'd been on the rifle team and won first place prize her freshman and sophomore years in the district shooting contest.

Randi's eyebrows rose, but she shook her head. "You were really good. And that would be a great suggestion if you didn't have a broken collarbone. I don't think they'd believe, even as good as you were, that you could hold and aim a shotgun."

"Dex broke his collarbone a couple of years ago. He'd never go for the lie." Mavis pulled a tattered vinyl kitchen chair closer and plopped her boots on the old coffee table.

Randi laughed. "Davie got bucked off when he was seventeen and broke his."

"I wonder if Drew has broken his." The words were out before she knew it and slapping her good hand over her mouth didn't force them back. "Not that I care. It was a general question." Now she was making it worse. They were going to think she was interested in Drew—or not. It was an innocent question after all if she didn't panic and make it worse.

"Dex told me Drew broke his when he was six, not long after their mom died." Mavis stood and walked to the kitchen. She came back with three glasses of iced tea. "Made fresh this morning with home grown tea."

Gina frowned. "What part of the Rafter D grows tea?"

"The tea gardens are right beside the quinoa groves." Randi's expression didn't change, but Gina could see the humor in her eyes.

"Are you hungry?" Mavis asked.

"Drew fixed me a sandwich. I'm really fine. I don't want to waste any more of your time. You can go home now."

"You might rethink that request when we show you what we brought along with the groceries." Randi stood and walked toward the kitchen.

Gina looked at Mavis but only got a shrug in response. She heard the sound of her freezer opening then closing and clanking coming from her silverware drawer.

Randi came back with a tray and set it on the table. She handed one of the Bennie's Burgers cups to Gina. Chocolate sprinkled vanilla ice cream towered above the cup with red cherry syrup floating around the rim. "Chocolate-covered-cherry Frostie. My favorite. How did you know?"

"We were hoping your tastes hadn't changed."

The room was quiet as the women dug into their icy desserts. As Gina scraped the last bits of chocolate from her cup, Randi just had to open her mouth. "So, you and Drew?"

The bite of ice cream Gina put in her mouth stuck in her throat. She did not want to have this conversation with these women—or anyone. After working hard all these years to keep her private life private, she wasn't about to share hard luck stories now. Best to pretend not to understand. "Me and Drew what? We're helping each other out."

"Right." Mavis drew the word out. "He's helping you drive and you're helping him—do what?"

Randi grinned.

"Look, I don't want anything from Drew. I don't want anything from any of you. I'm doing fine on my own." The old defensiveness she'd worked hard to corral broke free. Her heart raced, and she couldn't get enough air. "I think it's time for you to leave and not come back."

Mavis' grin faded. "Oh Gina. I'm sorry. I didn't mean

that. I was kidding."

Randi leaned forward and set her cup on the table. "After watching how much Abbie has hurt Drew, we're tickled to see him find some happiness. We're sorry if you thought we were making fun of you."

Closing her eyes, Gina turned her head away. She could smell the faint scent of Randi's citrus perfume and feel Mavis straightening her quilt. For years she'd waited for someone to show general concern for her. For someone to realize how hard she struggled.

The words were too little, too late. She knew the Dunbar wives were good people, but she couldn't afford to accept their friendship and then lose it again. Better to remain alone. "I really need a nap. Could you please close the door when you leave?"

She faked sleep as Randi and Mavis moved around the room putting it to order. The aroma of frying hamburger and tomato sauce let her know the women were making spaghetti sauce. She could make the Italian food last for a week if she was careful. As soon as she could get around, she'd send enough money to cover the cost of the meal.

At one time, the three women had been as close as the brothers, but circumstances and Gina's jealousy had ruined their friendship. In a short amount of time, it seemed they'd both moved on with their lives and forgotten all about her.

Mavis tiptoed into the living room and pulled the quilt up to Gina's chest. "Drew will be back in a half hour. We're going to head home. One of these days, we're going to be friends again. I'm sure of that."

At the sound of the back door clicking shut, Gina opened her eyes. She waited until she heard Mavis' car pull out of the driveway before she tried to get up. As she stared out the window, she saw the car turn the corner as the women drove back to the ranch.

The story of her life. Nothing that was good ever stuck around. Better to run them off than to be hurt again.

CHAPTER FIVE

"Did you get the pipes delivered?" That had been Gina's only question when he'd arrived at her house.

"No problem. Everything is taken care of." Except for her crashed truck and trailer, essentially her broken business, but he'd work on that in the morning.

With a sigh, she'd relaxed. "Good."

Thinking of the events of the evening before, he could still see her brows draw down into a frown as he'd handed her a wreath decorated with holly and tiny ornaments. Her reaction wasn't what he'd expected.

After staring at him for a long moment, she laid the wreath on the coffee table. She managed to get off the couch, and with a curt *goodnight*, she'd disappeared into the bedroom.

Christmas at the Dunbar house was always a joyous family affair. Even after his mother had died, Nana Lucy and his father had worked hard to make the holidays nice for the boys. What had happened to Gina to make her react the way she did?

At ten o'clock, he'd switched off the TV, hung the wreath on the back door, and curled up on the sofa for the night. No way was he leaving her alone whether she wanted him there or not.

As he scrambled eggs the next morning, she'd wandered out of her bedroom, dressed in a ratty, faded blue robe. Her eyes had widened in surprise at the sight of him. "Why are you still here?"

"Why hello, Drew. Thanks for helping me yesterday. What's for breakfast?" Drew grinned over his shoulder then returned to flipping the bacon strips. When she didn't answer, he turned to face her. "How are you feeling this morning?"

She sat in the kitchen chair, her good arm on the table and her head resting on her hand. Her words were muffled. "I'm sorry. Thanks for all you've done. I was surprised you didn't go home."

Drew dished up a plate and set it in front of her. "I'm not going to leave you alone while you're hurt." He retrieved his plate and sat across from her. "What do you have on the agenda for today?"

"I need to deliver a baler to the Foreman Ranch and a load of cement to the Taylors."

"Let me get Boomer and Fred fed, and I'll be ready to go."

"I don't know how I'll pay you, but I will."

"We'll worry about that later." Drew set his plate in the sink and hurried out the back door. She'd never know how much helping her was helping him. Otherwise, he'd be moping around the ranch, thinking of ways to kill Abbie.

A skiff of snow covered the ground. He reached out and shook the branches of the small tree, scattering snowflakes onto Fred's nose. The ancient Border Collie tried to bounce around then settled for a sharp bark. Old Man Winter was finally making his presence known in the area. The forecast called for more of the white stuff and well below freezing temperatures for the next couple of weeks.

Fred tagged along at Drew's heels. The dog had been Gina's inseparable companion since her senior year in high school. As he threw hay to the horse, Fred ran to the shed, his whines loud and frantic. He raced back to Drew and with a sharp bark ran to the shed again.

"What have you got there, buddy?" In the corner of the building lay an orange and black kitten, covered with slobber, its hair sticking out in pointy spikes. When he reached down, the tiny thing cringed. "There, there. I won't hurt you." He carefully picked it up and made his way back to the house.

Drew grabbed a dishtowel from the drawer and carried the kitten to where Gina sat in the living room. "To get you in the holiday mood, I brought you your first Christmas present. Couldn't wrap it though. The little thing wouldn't hold still long enough to get the ribbon on." He placed the calico on her lap.

"Oh, you poor thing." Gina picked up the corner of the towel and began cleaning the kitten. She looked at him. "Where did you find her?"

"Fred found her in the shed. Looks like she went a round or two with a neighborhood dog. I don't think anything's broken."

"She's skin and bones. I wonder who she belongs to."

"Whoever it is, doesn't deserve her. She looks like she hasn't had a good meal in a while." Drew grabbed a piece of bacon from breakfast and broke it into smaller pieces. When he laid it in front of the kitten, the fluffball growled and crouched over the meat.

"Do we need to take her to the vet?" Gina stroked one finger along the kitten's back, ignoring the growling.

"I don't think she's badly hurt, just hungry and banged up. We'll keep an eye on her." He poured a small bowl of milk and carried it into the living room. "Here you go. You're probably thirsty, too."

The kitten wolfed down the meat and lapped up all the milk. Her tiny tummy was round as she cleaned her face.

"What are you going to name her?" Drew watched as Gina's face softened.

"I don't care. You name her." Gina settled the little animal in her lap and stroked its bony back until the kitten fell asleep.

"How about if we wait and see what kind of name she chooses?" Drew got two cups of coffee from the kitchen and handed one to Gina. He settled on the other end of the couch and took a sip. "Want to tell me what happened?"

Gina focused her attention on the kitten before speaking. "I was between Mountain Home and Boise, passing a semi loaded with tires. Must have been a novice driver, because he lost control on the ice. Forced me off the road." Tears filled her eyes. "My truck's toast, every part of my body hurts, and my head feels like I've just gotten off a drunken twenty-four-hour roller-coaster ride. Even if I could find another truck and trailer, I can't drive."

"Well, darn it, Wally. You've got to learn to be more careful." He watched in amusement as a pink blush covered her cheeks. The best way to keep her from sinking into depression was to tease her.

"You know nothing about driving on these roads with an idiot behind the wheel of nearly every rig." She pulled in a deep breath and let it out slowly. "I'm sorry. I know you were only teasing."

"Now, do you want to tell me why you ran Mavis and Randi off? They were trying to help."

Gina studiously ignored the question and sipped at her coffee.

"You've made it clear you don't like them, but for the life of me, I can't understand why." Drew studied her face, the dark eyes and wide mouth. He managed to dredge up her smile from his memories. In high school, it was there often, but he'd only seen it a couple of times since he'd been home. "Unlike me, my brothers seem to have great taste in women."

Her attention focused on the kitten, and he knew

without her saying a word that she wasn't going to explain. "Never mind. Everybody has their reasons."

Gina swallowed and turned her gaze on him. The bruise beneath her eyes was turning yellow around the edges. "You'll think it's stupid."

"Do you still have a crush on Dex? Is that it? Jealousy?" A sharp pang shot through his heart at the thought of Gina pining away for his brother.

Her mouth fell open. "No! I haven't felt that way since middle school."

"Then what?"

Her eyes closed, and her body relaxed. With a sigh, she leaned back against the couch. "In a way, you were right about the jealousy. Only I wasn't jealous about their husbands. Life seems to give Randi and Mavis everything they've ever wanted. I don't know how they do it. In my world, they're the Good Luck Sisters, and I'm a female Clark Griswold."

Drew couldn't think of anything to say. He'd been having the same thoughts about his brothers even though he knew they'd gone through their own troubles to get where they were today. "Sounds reasonable enough to me, except you look a lot better than Chevy Chase."

She opened her eyes and stared at him. "Now you're patronizing me."

"No, I'm not. Can't you take anything I say at face value?" He stood and grabbed his truck keys. Butting his head against this wall wasn't getting him anywhere. "I'm going to the co-op to pick up the bags of cement. You'll be more comfortable here until everything is loaded."

She settled the kitten on the sofa beside her and tried to stand.

Drew placed a finger on her shoulder to get her attention. He'd prefer that she'd stay home and let him take care of all the work until she'd recovered, but it would be a cold day in the Sahara when Gina let anyone take care of her. "You're staying here with your new charge. I'll be back to pick you up when I'm done." Without thinking, he leaned in and kissed her cheek then hurried out before she had a chance to slug him with her good arm.

***

It had been ten days since the accident, and for the first time, Gina had slept through the night. She was growing stronger each day, but the frustration of letting someone else do her work made her grind her teeth.

Not to mention the kiss. Her mind wouldn't quit blowing it out of proportion. It had only been a quick peck on her cheek. Rationally, she knew he'd only meant it as a gesture of kindness, but the concussion seemed to have caused the rational part of her brain to lose its hold on reality.

Grudgingly, she admitted Drew was a lifesaver. He'd stepped up and taken care of her and her business. Not to mention the animals. Fred was embarrassingly in love with Drew and followed him everywhere. Even Cat liked him.

Thinking of the calico seemed to have called the little animal. She came dashing through the room. With the grace of a gazelle, she leapt onto the couch and raced along the back, screeching to a stop beside Gina's head. "Hey, little one. Wish I had your energy."

"Don't you think it's time to give her a name?"

Drew's deep voice caused the hairs on her arms to stand at attention, and her heart kicked into high gear. She pulled in a deep breath and kept her expression as neutral as she could manage. She'd die before she let him know how much he affected her. "Cat is a name."

He stared at Gina as if she hadn't a brain in her head. "How is Cat going to achieve her full potential with a generic name? How about Holly? Or, Stormy, because I found her after that little snowstorm?" When he reached out to pet the kitten, she swatted his hand and raced away at top speed.

Gina couldn't contain her laughter. "Okay, I know the perfect name. Missile."

"That's not bad, but I was kind of hoping for a holiday theme."

"Then she's officially Mistletoe. Missile for short."

"It was buried deep, but I knew you had some holiday spirit in you somewhere." Drew grinned, but a chill washed over Gina. She couldn't think of one good memory of Christmas. The days leading up to the 25th were filled with hope when she'd been young, but disappointment had hardened her heart. She'd learned early not to count on Santa Claus, the fickle bugger. It seemed he loved other kids more than her, and she'd spent years trying to figure out what she'd done wrong.

The kitten raced through the room like her tail was on fire then dropped into Drew's lap and proceeded to wash her face. Gina laughed out loud. To heck with Santa. Missile was the best present she'd ever gotten.

Drew stroked the kitten's fur with a long finger, and Gina felt a shiver run up her spine at the sight. She turned away and picked up her scheduling notebook off the table. Flipping through the pages, she cleared her throat. "You don't need to keep helping me, you know. I'm healing up just fine."

Drew chuckled and shifted the sleeping cat to the sofa before standing. "You're still having problems lifting a coffee cup. How are you going to shift your one-ton?"

He had her there. Using her arm was still a struggle. She'd always relied on a sarcastic answer when she was embarrassed, but this time she bit back a retort. Drew had been nothing but kind, and she wasn't going to repay him with snark.

"You're right." She stepped out the back door and turned.

Before she could say another work, he broke in. "Wait—what. Say that again. I couldn't have heard you right."

Her heart gave a jolt at the sight of his grin, and all the

fun went out of their exchange. She wasn't getting involved with this man. With any man. "Come on then." She tossed him the keys and hurried toward the truck. "You're driving."

An icy blast of wind whipped her breath away as she climbed into the passenger seat. After slamming the door, Gina struggled to get the seatbelt hooked.

Without a word, Drew reached across and fastened it for her.

She looked up to say thanks and saw the big grin on his face. Her plan had been to keep this strictly business between them as long as she needed his help. Her friendships with the other Dunbar brothers hadn't ended well, and she didn't see anything better happening with Drew. He was still married for goodness sake.

His smile though. It made things seem better. Wouldn't she ever learn? Apparently not. "You going to get on the road, or are we going to sit here and make googly eyes?"

Drew straightened his spine and stuck out his chest. "I don't make googly eyes. That's for girls. I'm giving you a manly glower."

Forget the smile. She laughed out loud until her stomach hurt. As she wiped her eyes, she glanced at Drew. He stuck out his tongue then hit the ignition and pulled slowly away from the front of her house.

They drove in silence for a while, but she couldn't seem to get the damned grin to leave her face, and that was a problem. Her life was so much happier with Drew in it. He'd made her laugh more in the last few weeks than she had in years. If it wasn't for the little voice in the back of her mind, insisting she face the truth—and the truth was Drew wouldn't stay—her life would be perfect. She turned her gaze to the side window and watched the frost covered sagebrush as the desert scenery rushed by.

Drew's voice brought her back from her daydreams. "I'd like to ask you something."

When she nodded, he continued. "If you don't feel like

answering, I'll understand."

Her jaw tightened. The qualification let her know she wasn't going to like where this conversation was heading, but she nodded again. Holding all her secrets inside was damn hard, and tiring. Drew wouldn't tell anyone else, of that she was sure. And, it wasn't like he'd stay around here anyway. As soon as Abbie crooked her finger, he'd be off again.

"What have you got against Christmas?"

"I don't like fat men with beards."

STEPHANIE BERGET

CHAPTER SIX

The annual Christmas tree harvesting trip the day after Thanksgiving had been filled with as many laughs and mishaps as usual, maybe more with Mavis and Randi joining in. His brothers had set up the trees at Nana Lucy's and Dex's houses, and they'd spent the evening decorating and eating Nana's fresh Christmas cookies and fruitcake.

Most people joked about fruitcake, but the delectable delicacy his grandmother baked was a treat he looked forward to each year. He'd grabbed two loaves before everyone scarfed them down and wrapped them up to take to Gina.

The drive to Homedale was beautiful this morning. Gina had refused his invitation to have Thanksgiving at the Rafter D, but he was going to try one more time to get her in the holiday spirit. He'd wanted to bring her along when they'd searched for the trees, but she'd emphatically refused that, too.

Drew knew he should drop it, but he couldn't bear to watch the sad look on her face as everyone else prepared for the holidays. He pulled into her driveway and sat for a moment, gathering his thoughts.

The wreath still hung on her back door where he'd put

it. At least she hadn't taken it down. That was good, right?

Pushing the wreath to one side, he looked through the window. Gina sat at the kitchen table with a steaming cup of something and Missile in her lap. With a short rap, he opened the door and dragged a small blue-green tree into the back room. "Brought you a present."

The small smile faded from Gina's face. Shaking her head, she stood. "What have you got?"

"This, my dear, is a baby Juniper. It's not the most perfectly shaped Christmas tree, but it was available, and I like the color." Drew carried the tree into the living room along with a stand he'd dug out from the storage above the barn. He slid the small rocker to the side and placed the tree in the corner in front of the picture window. "Perfect size if I do say so myself."

"That's so nice of you Drew, but I don't have any decorations. Maybe you could donate it to the shelter somewhere."

Drew watched as she crossed the room and ran a hand down the branches.

"Really thanks, but …"

Ignoring her protests, he hurried out to the truck and carried in the box he'd brought from Nana Lucy's basement. The overhead light caused the shiny ornaments to glitter. "Mavis and Randi picked out these from the boxes of extras at the ranch. I don't think Nana Lucy has ever gotten rid of a decoration in her life." He picked up a barrel racer ornament. "Mavis found this at the gift shop in town and wanted me to give it to you."

Gina's eyes filled with tears, and she ran to the bedroom.

Christmas decorations were supposed to be happy things. Looks like he'd blown it again. The last thing he'd wanted to do was make this woman cry. He hesitated then walked to the bedroom door. He had to make this right. He just wasn't sure how.

Gina sat on her bed, a tissue in her hands. She didn't

meet his eyes. "Sorry." The one short word was filled all the pain she obviously held inside.

"If anyone's sorry, it's me. I wanted to bring a little Christmas spirit into your life, and it looks like my plan was an epic fail." Drew sat beside her and put his arm around her stiff shoulders.

She leaned her head against him. "When I was a little kid, I never knew which mom was going to appear around Christmas. One of them was normal." She tilted her head and gave him a watery smile. "Well, as normal as Helen Wallace ever got."

"I remember your mom. She was quirky, but she didn't seem so bad."

"She hid it well. There was an angry, jealous, demanding woman inside. She blamed everyone, but mostly me for the way her life turned out." Gina blew her nose then settled against Drew again. "I don't remember one Christmas morning when she didn't throw a fit and destroy everything except for the one where she was dead level drunk by six a.m."

Drew pulled her into his arms, his heart breaking for the trauma this woman had survived.

"She even set the tree on fire the year I was twelve. I got it out before the house burned down, but the one present she'd wrapped for me was ruined." She sniffed. "That was the last tree we ever got."

"We're starting a new tradition with new rules. And I can't believe I'm going to say this, but here's the first rule. Number one—no violence at Christmas." Drew stood and pulled her to her feet. "This will be the first tree for the rest of your life." He led her into the living room and handed her the box of ornaments. "You look through these while I get the lights and tinsel." He hurried out the door before she could respond. Maybe he could give her one great holiday before he went back to figuring out his crappy life.

They spent the next few hours decorating and laughing.

Gina seemed to enjoy listening to his stories of growing up on the ranch. Her best memories seemed to come from her high school years.

When they took a break, Gina made toasted cheese sandwiches. They'd settled onto the couch with the food and a beer when Drew's phone rang. He looked at the caller ID and groaned. Swiping, he said, "Hey, man. I hope this is good news for a change."

His lawyer's laugh wasn't filled with humor.

"It's not the worst news. Abbie has cut her demands. She only wants half of your half of the ranch."

Drew dropped his head against the back of the couch and sighed. "You know that's not possible."

"You might consider her offer. It's the best one yet."

"Not even for a minute. The ranch belongs to my family. Can you imagine what kind of hell she'd make their lives if she had anything to say about the running of the Rafter D?" Drew said goodbye and closed his eyes. How had he been so fooled by his wife? Almost ex-wife if he could convince her to forget about the ranch. His naivety was going to cost his whole family.

"What can I do to help?"

Drew felt a soft touch on his arm and opened his eyes to see Gina's blue ones filled with concern. "I don't think anyone can help me. I'm my own worst enemy."

Gina set her plate on the coffee table and turned to him. "You want me to find her and beat her up?" She raised her thin arm and flexed her bicep. "They call me The Homedale Hitman."

Despite his frustration, Drew couldn't stop a smile from spreading across his face. He didn't have a doubt that Gina could take Abbie out, and he imagined the scenario for a moment before pulling himself back to reality. He tried to lighten the moment. "You might ruin your manicure."

Gina jerked her arm down and glared at him. "Looks like you're mistaking me for that money-grubbing wife of yours." She stood and strode out of the room, and he heard her banging pots around in the kitchen.

He wanted to take offense, but he knew she was right. No way would Gina let nail polish interfere with something she wanted.

Abbie wouldn't either. She'd con someone else into doing the dirty work.

As he stood to follow her and apologize, his cell rang again. When he looked at the caller ID, his heart dropped. He almost stuffed the darned thing back in his pocket. Refusing to answer the call wouldn't solve anything, and she'd call back. "What?"

"Hi, baby. I missed you."

Abbie must have been practicing her country twang because it was much more pronounced than the last time Drew had talked to her. He'd used to love her voice. Now the phony sound grated on his nerves. The day he was finally done with this woman would be the best of his life. He waited without speaking, sure she'd fill the silence.

He wasn't wrong.

"You're quiet today. Have you been working too hard on that big old ranch?" Her soft giggle used to set his heart on fire. Now it irritated him.

"What do you want?" Drew pulled in a deep breath and tried to calm his nerves. Maybe she'd come to her senses and would handle the divorce with some class. "My attorney said you'd lowered your demands. You have to know I won't give up any part of the ranch."

Her sexy sigh came through the phone loud and clear, and Drew wondered if she practiced that, too.

"I've been thinking. My attorney doesn't want us talking, but I think if we meet face to face, we can work things out. I'll be in Boise to sign a contract next Wednesday. Can you meet me?"

This was another one of Abbie's attempts to manipulate him. He was almost sure of it, but on the small chance she was serious, he had to take the chance. "Where and when?"

"Oh, Drew. I knew we could figure out a solution if we tried. We've always gotten along."

"As long as I did what you said," Drew muttered. While he jotted down the specifics, he looked up to see Gina watching from the doorway.

She shook her head, turned on her heel, and left the house.

***

It hadn't taken Drew long to leave the night before. In the back of her mind, Gina had hoped he'd come find her in the barn and tell her she was wrong.

He hadn't even bothered to say goodbye.

The sun was barely above the horizon when she threw the hay in the feeder. Leaning both forearms on the top rail of her horse's pen, she watched the bay eat.

Missile scampered through the scattering of snow around her boots before climbing the post to sit on the shoulder of her jacket. Fred shuffled over and leaned against her leg.

Reaching up, she stroked a hand down the kitten's back. "Well, guys, today's the big day. Drew is going back to that nasty lady." Fred nudged her and gave her a doggy smile. "I know. It was nice having him around for a while, but we all knew it wouldn't last."

At the sound of tires on gravel, she turned to see Drew's pickup pull to a stop by her house. As he made his way across the barnyard, she took her last chance to enjoy to the sight of Wranglers encasing his long legs.

He stopped beside her and leaned against the fence. After giving Fred a scratch, he met her eyes.

"I thought you'd be on your way to Boise by now. What time is your date with Abigail?" She struggled to keep the tension out of her voice. She'd never been very good at nonchalance or hiding her feelings. Or very good at much of anything.

"That's why I'm here." He stared at the toes of his boots like a kid caught with his hand in the candy jar.

When he lifted his gaze, she noticed the stubble on his cheeks. She thought back but couldn't remember a time when Drew wasn't clean-shaven. He must be more upset than she'd thought about this meeting.

"Will you come with me?"

For once in her life, Gina was speechless. He was going to meet with his wife and asking her to ride along? Who did that? She stuffed her fingers in the pockets of her jeans before making her way to the frost covered lawn chairs.

Drew followed her.

She brushed the frost off with one gloved hand before she sat down. "Why one earth would I go see Abbie with you?" Gina felt her cheeks warm with embarrassment although she couldn't figure out why she should be embarrassed. This was squarely on Drew's shoulders.

"You don't owe me anything. I have this feeling she's up to something, and I want a witness." A small smile spread across his lips. "And maybe a hit man."

And just like that, she felt the anger drain away. She could be a witness, in fact, she might really enjoy the look on Abbie's face when she saw Drew wasn't alone. She snuck a look at him below lowered lashes. A sigh almost escaped. The man was everything she'd ever dreamed of—smart, kind, and oh so good looking. She stuffed the dreams away in the corner of her heart. This wasn't the time for letting her fantasies out.

Besides, Drew was right about one thing. Abbie had ulterior motives in arranging this meet-up.

"Look, I know this puts you in a bad position. Forget I said anything."

Gina realized she hadn't answered him, only glared. Her expression relaxed. "You know, I haven't seen Abbie for a few years. I'd like to chat about old times." Her grin widened.

Drew watched her, confusion on his face. "You scare me sometimes."

"Me? Little old me? I'm a sweetheart. You know that." She waggled her eyebrows at him then took a step toward the house before turning. "Want some coffee while I change my clothes?"

With Drew settled at the kitchen table, she went through her closet. What to wear to meet the almost ex-wife? In the back, she spied a clothing box. She pulled out the thin, red wool dress that Gladys had given her for her last birthday. It hugged her body like it had been custom made. With a V-neck, and long sleeves, it had a holiday feel and was flattering. It was also the only pretty thing she owned.

With a sigh, she folded it back into the box. Even at her best, she couldn't compete with Abbie. Starched jeans and a cobalt blue shirt were her next choice, but they didn't seem right either. She sank onto the bed before flopping onto her back. Who was she trying to kid? She wasn't in Abbie's class no matter what she wore. A devious idea popped into her head. Yup, she had the perfect outfit.

She dressed and pulled her long hair into a messy bun, and this hairstyle on her epitomized the word messy.

As she entered the kitchen, the look on Drew's face told her she'd achieved her goal.

"I thought you were going with me." Drew stood, poured the rest of his coffee into the sink, and rinsed his cup.

"I am." She pulled on the mud crusted work boots by the back door. "I'm ready if you are."

Drew stared at her dirty jeans and the University of Idaho sweatshirt with bits of hay decorating the shoulders. "Okay then. Let's hit the road."

They'd made small talk on the drive to Boise, and Drew hadn't mentioned her outfit again. Abbie hadn't arrived at the coffee shop yet so they ordered and chose a table in the back.

As they discussed the loads Gina had for the coming week, they heard a disturbance. Abbie swept in the door, smiling and waving. A little over the top, but Gina wasn't surprised. She shifted her gaze to Drew to see his reaction.

He stared, his jaw hard and his fists clenched. As she watched, he physically relaxed and pasted a small smile on his face. What was it costing him to appear unaffected?

Abbie caught sight of them and her smile faded for a second before she caught herself. She paused to sign a napkin for a fan before making her way to them.

"Hi, baby." She bent and kissed Drew's cheek. "Why did you bring your little friend? I thought we were going to talk about private matters." She slid into the chair across from them and made a show of flipping her hair over her shoulders and fluffing the skirt of her sexy sundress.

Really, a sundress in December, in the snow?

"Gina is my business partner. She has a right to hear about anything to do with the ranch, and I'm assuming that's what you're here for."

The shock on Abbie's face was comical, and the words slipped out of Gina's mouth before she could contain them. "I'm buying Drew's part of the ranch. Well, trading it for my trucking business."

Abbie whirled toward Drew. "You'd never sell the ranch."

Gina thought she'd stomped her high-heel clad foot beneath the table. She had to give Drew credit. He barely paused before answering her. "The Rafter D belongs to my brothers and their wives. I'd be a third wheel. I want to do something completely different anyway. When Gina came up the idea of a trade, I found it interesting."

"I don't believe you." She glared at Drew before turning her scorn on Gina. "And, what will you do on the ranch. Oh, I forgot. It doesn't bother you to be a third wheel. You've been one all your life."

The comment stung, and normally she'd have retaliated. Not today. This was about Drew. "Seems to me this isn't any of your business. You're divorcing him."

Whirling back to Drew, Abbie made an effort to corral her anger. "Baby, you don't really want to do this. Gina wants to get her hooks into the ranch. She thinks she'll be able to get Dex to look at her again."

Abbie knew how to push her buttons. The woman was devious.

Then again, Gina had been raised by the queen of sarcasm. She leaned closer and kissed Drew on the cheek before turning back to the woman. "I don't need Dex, sweetie. I have Drew."

While Abbie watched, her mouth open, Gina ran her hand through Drew's hair and kissed him on the lips. The chair screeched against the linoleum as Abbie stood and stormed out of the coffee shop.

Gina turned to Drew and smiled. "I think that went well."

CHAPTER SEVEN

Drew ended the call and sighed. It was the first week in December and they hadn't made any headway with the divorce. His attorney had informed him Abbie wanted all of his part of the ranch again. Any deal she'd offered was off.

Not that he'd ever considered giving her any of the ranch, but now she was out for blood.

When he had told the attorney what Gina had done, the man had laughed out loud. Then he'd half-heartedly scolded them for making things worse.

Drew continued saddling his horse. He'd finally talked Gina into coming to the ranch to ride through the heifers. The weather had been mild for the last couple of days, and he was looking forward to the ride. He suspected Gina had agreed because Mavis and Randi wouldn't be coming along, He didn't care what the reason was. He enjoyed Gina's company and her dry sense of humor.

He was still laughing about the trick she'd pulled on Abbie. Her attorney had been adamant that Drew not trade with Gina. Abbie wanted to be able to hold the ranch over Drew and his family.

Gina's truck and trailer pulled up to the barn, and she

hopped out and unloaded her horse. Drew rode over and waited while she checked her cinch and mounted. She looked around before smiling. "Where to?"

"Checking to see if Mavis or Randi is hiding?"

That was exactly what she'd been doing. She was too embarrassed to admit it, so she waited for him to make the next move. Relief swamped her when he didn't push the comment.

"Just over the hill on our right." Drew took the lead, and they rode in silence for a while.

Finally, she urged her horse into a trot until she'd pulled up next to him. "What's the latest on the diva?"

"Not good, as you've probably suspected." He grinned to soften the news. "She wants everything again."

Gina's expression fell. "Oh, no. Me and my big mouth have screwed everything up. I'm so sorry, Drew."

"It doesn't make any difference if she wants half of my part of the ranch or all of it. I'm not prepared to give her any. Besides, it was worth anything to see her expression when you kissed me."

In the two hours they'd spent checking cows, he couldn't get Gina to stop apologizing. When they'd completed the ride and reached the ranch again, they tied the horses up. Gina moved to stand in front of him. As she opened her mouth in what Drew was sure was another apology, he took her by the shoulders and kissed her to stop the words.

He'd meant it as a joke but found he couldn't stop the kiss.

She pulled back, looking into his eyes.

He'd thought she would run away, but she wound her arms around his neck and kissed him right back.

Holy cow! Abbie could learn a thing or two about kissing from this woman. And he'd be sure to tell her the next time he saw her. Then all thoughts of Abbie disappeared, and he fell into the kiss.

At the sound of someone tiptoeing past, Gina's body

stiffened, and she jerked away. He tightened his hold and turned his head to see Mavis moving through the barn door.

"Don't let me bother you. I'm just getting my horse." She grinned before disappearing.

A pretty pink blush covered Gina's neck and cheeks as he pulled her into a hug. Her stiff body gradually relaxed.

"There's nothing to be embarrassed about. This is between you and me and has nothing to do with anyone else. If you don't want me to kiss you again, say so." He touched her cheek. "I'm hoping you don't tell me to stop."

She stood on her toes and kissed his cheek. "Let me think." Then she untied her horse, loaded him in the trailer, and drove away.

Drew stood in the barnyard, watching the truck and trailer pull down the driveway. He'd heard the words gob smacked before. Now he knew the literal meaning.

A soft chuckle cut into his reverie, and he turned to find Mavis leading her horse to the hitching rail.

"That was interesting." She walked over to him and put her arm around his waist. "Just a friendly little kiss for a friend?"

Drew took a step back. "I love you Mavis, but this isn't any of your business." He could imagine how Gina would react if Mavis and Randi said anything about the kiss. He'd never get another one, and he knew that for a fact.

Mavis made a locking motion in front of her lips and tossed away the pretend key. "Nobody will hear about this from me. I'm pulling for both of you." Her smile faded. "Any news on the divorce?"

Drew dropped onto the worn bench in front of the barn. "Abbie wanted to meet. I'm sure she thought she could talk me into giving her what she wanted."

"You didn't give in, did you?" Mavis' expression of concern changed to apprehension.

"It didn't turn out exactly as Abbie had planned. I took Gina with me."

Mavis' laugh filled the barnyard. "Bet Miss Priss didn't like you bringing along back-up one bit. How's she supposed to blind you with her charm with Gina there?"

Drew dropped his face into his hands for a moment before raising his gaze to look at his sister-in-law. "I'm possibly the dumbest man in the world. Why couldn't I see Abbie for who she is?"

Mavis sat beside him and leaned against the faded red paint on the side of the barn. "Because you're a good person, and you didn't realize she wasn't."

"Everyone else saw through her theatrics."

"Give yourself a break. You loved her. Love is blind, yada, yada, yada." Mavis stood. "Come on. I'll help you put your horse away, then we'll go to the house for ice cream."

As they made their way to the house, Drew laughed. "Nana Lucy isn't going to give us ice cream before dinner."

Mavis grinned back. "Then we won't tell her." She took Drew's hand and pulled him toward the small shed off the back porch of Nana Lucy's house. She held her finger to her lips and carefully opened the faded wooden door.

A harvest gold freezer stood in the back corner.

Drew couldn't remember a time the appliance hadn't been there. Mavis opened the freezer door and pulled out a box of ice cream sandwiches. "We don't need a bowl or spoon to eat these.

"Knowing Nana, she's kept count of exactly what's in here. She'd going to know if some are missing."

Mavis snorted then pressed her hand over her mouth to keep from laughing. When she finally regained control, she leaned close to Drew's ear. "It's possible she thinks Dex steals the ice cream. Someone might have told her that." She grinned. "I'm not sure who would do such a dastardly thing."

"She'll give him hell."

"She already has, but the same someone told her he's

kind of depressed, and the ice cream makes him feel better."

"Well then, give me a couple more. If being depressed gets extra ice cream, I deserve the whole box." Drew meant the words, but as soon as they were out of his mouth, he realized he wasn't nearly as sad as he had been. Must have been the kiss. Gina had melted into his arms, and he was going to get her to do that again.

"What are you thinking about? You've got the goofiest grin on your face. Kind of like when Davie finally admitted he loved Randi." Mavis stood back with her hands on her hips. "Yes, that's exactly who you look like."

Drew stuffed the last bite of his ice cream into his mouth and chewed. He held up on finger, asking Mavis to wait while he finished. "The only problem is Gina doesn't love me."

"You truly are a dumb shit. She definitely loves you. She just hasn't admitted it to herself yet. Randi did the same thing." A tiny smile crossed Mavis' face as she nodded.

"I think you're getting ahead of things. We need to give Gina some time." Drew pushed against the freezer door to make sure it was fully closed before turning back to Mavis.

Her smile faded as her brows drew down into a frown. She glared at him as if he were an addle-brained calf. "We need to give Gina a kick in the rear. You've wasted years on that imbecile you married, and Gina's been alone too long."

"Are you sure?" Drew shook his head. "I mean about Gina being alone. Not the imbecile part. Those are years I'll never get back."

"You doubt my advice? I'm always right. Ask Dex."

Drew followed Mavis out of the freezer room then pulled the door closed. "Not sure he's the person to go to for an unbiased opinion."

"There are a couple of things we need to do before we begin Operation Love Gina. First, you need to get divorced—like yesterday."

"And the second one?"

"We need to figure out a way to get Gina to not hate me and Randi. Not sure she'd take our advice right now."

***

Gina had read the same article in the Homedale newspaper at least five times and still didn't have any idea what it said. Every time she let her attention wander the kiss filled her mind. She'd never been affected by a kiss like Drew's before. Not that she'd kissed many men, but still...

She thunked the heel of her hand against her forehead. There she went again. What was she going to do with herself? Drew was still married, and even if he had been single, he was way out of her league. She was only a pleasant interlude, an amusing diversion while he figured out what to do about Abbie.

She'd do herself a big favor if she remembered that.

Missile was draped over her lap, sound asleep. Folding the paper, she dropped it to the floor then ran her fingers down the kitten's soft fur. "Time for me to get going, Missy." Sliding her hands beneath the little body, she moved Missile to the pillow and stood. She'd go broke if she spent her days mooning over a man.

The kitten stretched, showing its little claws, then relaxed into sleep again.

"You've got the life there, little one." Gina checked the clock on her phone then hurried toward the door. Time to make some money so she could pay her bills.

She'd just turned onto Owyhee Ave to head to her next delivery when she heard the blaring sound of a truck's horn. As she pulled to the curb, Drew parked behind her. She rolled down the window as he came alongside.

His jaw was tight and his fist, where it rested on the edge of the window, was clenched.

She had to tamp down the urge to place her palm against his cheek. "What's wrong?" Gina turned the key to shut off her engine. "Has something happened to your family?" She placed her hand over his and felt it relax slightly.

"It's Abbie. More of the same I'm sad to say. I was wondering if I could ride along with you. I need to fill you in on the latest with the witchy woman." She nodded, and he walked around to climb into the passenger seat.

When they'd driven out of town, Drew cleared his throat. "She's stooped to a new low. She says if you and I trade, she's going to take your business, plus sue me for the ranch."

"I'd like to see her try. She couldn't keep my customers. All she'd end up with is a truck and trailer. Not worth her time." Gina felt the smile spread across her face as she pictured Abbie driving her rig.

"That's not all. She says she's going to sue you for alienation of affection."

"What affection?" Gina's smile turned into an all-out laugh. "You and me?"

"She's already filed the paperwork. She's accusing you of causing the divorce." Drew's expression fell even further.

All the humor fled as her lungs refused to expand. "She can't win, can she?"

"My attorney says it's unlikely she'll be able to get a judge to give her all she wants, but he can't guarantee she won't get some part. You never know about the courts."

Gina pulled into the Crawford place and turned off the engine. Matt Crawford already had his boys out there to unload the irrigation pipe.

By the time they'd exchanged pleasantries and gossiped about the neighbors, the young men were done. Drew shook Matt's hand then they made their way back home.

Gina's thoughts whirled, and she couldn't keep track of Drew's attempt at conversation. She knew Abbie's chances of succeeding on this latest vindictive venture were slim, but her reputation would be shredded.

Most of the people she knew would assume she'd broken up Abbie's marriage. Sweet Abbie Anjelica. With Abbie's growing popularity, this fiasco might even be on the front page of the tabloids. For a shy, private person, having her personal life aired before the world would be a living hell.

She stopped under the big tree by her barn and turned to Drew. "I can't do this. I can't see you anymore." Without another word, she climbed out and made her way to the house. Hopefully, Drew would take a hint and leave her alone.

The hinge on the back door told her he wouldn't to do as she wanted. "We have to fight this."

She stood in the middle of the living room, her back to him. "I mean it, Drew. She probably won't win on either suit, I know that, but I can't have the rest of the town thinking I'll take any Dunbar brother no matter the cost."

She felt Drew as he came closer. "No one would believe that."

"They already do. Remember the day at the bank after I'd hauled Abbie's car in? When Mary stormed by us, she was mad because she wanted to date you and thought I was already worming my way in. She'll have rumors spread all over town within minutes of hearing about the lawsuit."

Drew stood behind her. Wrapping his arms around her shoulders, he pulled her against his broad chest. He rested his chin on the top of her head. "I don't care what the people of this town say, but it's obvious you do. This town means nothing to me. You mean everything. We could leave the area."

Gina had relaxed into his warmth, but at his words, she pulled away. "Your family is here. Your home is here." She touched his cheek with her fingers before pulling her hands away. "I can't do this. You'd end up regretting it."

"I would never regret being with you."

Gina looked at him for the last time. "You have to go. Please don't come back. I don't want to see you anymore."

Watching Drew drive away was one of the hardest things Gina had ever done but letting him stay would only bring her more heartache, and she'd had enough of that to last a lifetime.

The following weeks without his nearly daily appearances were empty. She'd spent most of the time watching mindless sitcoms or staring out the window. The weather had turned cold and snowy. Her business slowed considerable in the winter, and she had nothing to do but think.

When the rumor got back to her that Dex had dragged Drew out of the Jordan Valley bar when he'd tried to pick a fight, Gina knew she had to do something.

The phone call to Mavis was short and sweet. When her former friends pulled into the driveway Gina nearly turned and ran. She pinched the bridge of her nose and pulled in a deep breath. Throwing back her shoulders, she straightened her spine. The days of being a coward were over.

She'd made a pot of Seattle's MarketSpice tea, her favorite cold weather drink. Reaching into the top shelf of the cupboard, she pulled out a delicate china plate. With an index finger, she touched one of the tiny roses woven in a pattern around the edge.

When she'd found the plate at a resale store, she'd bought it on a whim. She'd loved the elegant look. So different from most of the things in her life.

After arranging half a package of Oreos in concentric circles on the plate, she placed one of the antique ornaments from her tree in the center. She couldn't remember her mother ever entertaining a women friend, and this was as close as she could come to hospitality.

After a quick knock, Mavis and Randi swept into the kitchen along with a gust of icy wind.

"About time you came to your senses and remembered

we were friends." Mavis gave her a quick hug and even though Gina stiffened, the smile remained on Mavis' face.

"I'm hoping this is a war council to determine the best way to get rid of Abbie." Randi picked up a cookie and looked at Gina as she took a bite. "Mind if I pour the tea?"

Memories of when these two were her best friends flooded back, and Gina could only nod in agreement. She took the mug Randi held out, picked up the plate of cookies, and led the way to the living room.

When they were all seated, Randi grinned. "I wasn't kidding about the war council."

Tears burned at the back of Gina's eyes, but with sheer willpower, she pushed them down. She managed to keep her voice steady, and her attitude unconcerned. "I can't get involved in that. I wanted to let you know I'm moving to Vale, Oregon."

Both women stared at her. Finally, Mavis shook her head. "You can't let Abbie run you out."

Gina stuffed a cookie into her mouth, giving her a moment to form her reply.

Randi handed her another one. "Take your time. I want to hear this."

Leave it to Randi to add a little levity. Gina relaxed enough to swallow. She took a drink of tea then placed the cup carefully on the table. "I asked you here because I'm worried about Drew."

"You're not running because you're worried Abbie will take your business? We won't let that happen." Mavis stood and walked to the window. Her back was still to them when she spoke. "We are going to take that woman down. I don't know how, but the three of us can do it."

Gina shook her head. "Here's what I know. If I'm gone, Abbie may back off. I insulted her, and she's not going to forget that." When Randi opened her mouth to speak, Gina held up her hand. "I'm also worried about what the people of this town will say when Abbie sues me for alienation of affection."

Randi snorted.

Gina whirled to face her. "Can you honestly tell me you didn't think I wanted to take Dex from Mavis?"

A blush crept up Randi's cheeks.

"Can you imagine what it will be like when this shit hits the fan? People will snicker behind my back. I can take it, but can you imagine what they'll say about Drew. I can't do that to him." Gina sank down on the sofa, and she kept her gaze on the women.

Mavis sat beside her. "Drew misses you. He's miserable."

"He'll get over it. And, he'd be more miserable if I stayed."

STEPHANIE BERGET

CHAPTER EIGHT

The week leading up to Christmas wasn't the best time of year to find a new place to live. Everyone else was in the holiday spirit and not concerned with mundane things.

Because Gina had made up her mind to start the new year anywhere but Homedale, she kept up the search. Vale, Oregon, would be the perfect place. More than half of her regular customers lived on the Oregon side of the border, and with a small amount of advertising and word of mouth, she'd pick up new ones.

In the only stroke of luck she'd had for years, she heard through coffee shop gossip that one of her regular customers had five acres with a small house. The acreage also contained a shop larger than she needed. He had been waiting for spring to remodel before putting the place up for sale. After a few negotiations, she convinced him to sell now.

She'd put in an offer and was now a homeowner. In a matter of a few days, her life had changed.

At noon on Christmas Eve she found herself standing in the bank, waiting for a teller. First, she needed to close out her business account at the Homedale bank. As she waited, she ran through the mental list of other chores to be completed before she loaded up and moved.

"Gina!" A voice cut through her musings, and she looked up to see Mary waving at her. There was a smile on the teller's face, even though her expression didn't hold an ounce of friendliness.

Gina slid her checkbook across the counter. "I need to close this account, please."

"You're leaving us?" Mary opened the checkbook. "What's going on?"

Gina didn't want to have this conversation with Mary, but short of being rude, she couldn't think of a way to stop it. "I'm moving to Vale. I bought a house over there."

In a voice loud enough to the other patrons to hear, Mary said, "Congratulations!" Leaning across the counter, the teller lowered her voice to just above a whisper. "I told you the Dunbar brothers were out of your league. I hear Abbie is suing you. Moving to Vale isn't going to save you from trying to steal Drew from her."

Gina snatched the checkbook out of Mary's hands and hurried out of the bank.

As the door swung shut, she heard Mary's laugh. She nearly ran to her truck, sliding inside. The nasty teller had probably already told everyone she knew about the lawsuit. And the story would be embellished until even Abbie wouldn't recognize it.

She slammed the truck into gear then took a breath to try and calm her pounding heart. Pulling onto the road, she drove home. It was time to pack, time to escape.

As she sat in the driveway, she could see Mary's mocking face as if the woman was right in front of her.

At one time, she'd had lots of friends in this town. Dropping her forehead to rest against the steering wheel, she let the memories wash over her. The faces of her friends appeared in her mind, especially Randi and Mavis. She realized she'd been the one to pull away.

She'd isolated herself.

Climbing out of the truck, she walked to the road.

Leaning against her dented, rusty mailbox, she took a long look at her neighbor's homes. The Caldwell boy still mowed her lawn without asking for money. Gran Carter brought her an apple pie every Halloween, and Mason Tanner plowed her drive whenever the snow got over a couple of inches.

Many others had remained friendly even when she hadn't been. As she thought back to her mother, she realized she was following in the woman's footsteps. Her mother had become more reclusive the older she'd gotten.

Sadly, there had only been a handful of people at her funeral.

As Gina walked back to her house, a sense of calm wrapped around her for the first time in forever. The truth became clear. How she reacted to the rumors and gossip was totally her choice. The only important person was Drew, and she'd pushed him away without giving him a chance.

People could talk, and she could ignore all of them. All except man she loved.

Gina didn't know if Drew would be able to do the same. If she walked away now, without finding out, she'd spend the rest of her life wondering if she'd thrown away her dream life.

She plugged in the small tree Drew had helped her decorate. She touched the barrel racer ornament Mavis and Randi had given her. How had she ignored the friendship others had offered? It was time to make that right.

She made a short phone call then a quick trip to the drug store for makeup and a jar of scented lotion. After a shower, she blew her hair dry. As she dug out her old curling iron, she hoped the thing still worked. She hadn't done more than pull her hair into a thick braid for years. The makeup took longer to apply than she remembered. It was another thing she hadn't used in years.

Finally, she dug into her closet and pulled out the starched jeans she kept for the few times she needed to dress up. Jeans would have to do.

The clothing box sat in the bottom of her closet right where she'd left it. The red dress Gladys had given her still had the tags on it. At the time she'd considered the bright color to be too much, but it was perfect for the new and improved Gina Wallace.

She held it in front of her as she looked in the mirror. The color brightened her blue eyes and looked great with her skin and hair. Slipping it over her head, she let it settle around her body.

The soft knit hugged her curves. When she raised her gaze to the mirror again, she couldn't believe her eyes. A pretty sexy woman looked back. She did a slow twirl. Not half bad. Time to go find Drew.

Missile raced in front of her as she moved to the back door. Reaching down, she lifted the kitten into her arms. "I know you like to go with me, but this is something I have to do for myself."

When she set the kitten on the floor, the little thing ran to the back door and meowed. The big blue eyes studied her before looking at the door again.

Gina picked her up and scratched her under her chin. "Okay, baby. I don't think they'll mind another person for Christmas." She pulled open the back door, Missile cradled in her arm to find Drew standing on the back porch, his hand lifted to knock.

Dressed in starched Wranglers and a pressed western shirt, he nearly made her mouth water. She looked into his eyes, and on impulse, she leaned forward and kissed him.

"Now, that's a Christmas greeting I love. Mind if I come in?" His grin made her heart race and she struggled to control her breathing.

Stepping back, she made room for him to enter.

Drew took the kitten from her arms and without another word, he pulled her into his. Warmth spread over her as his lips touched hers, and she melted against him. He leaned away before saying, "We need to talk."

She'd always thought talking was over-rated, so she lifted the piece of mistletoe she had clutched in the hand and held it over his head. "It's bad luck to ignore mistletoe." This kiss held all her unspoken emotions.

"I wouldn't call that talking, but I like it." Drew took her hand and led her to the sofa. When he pulled her onto his lap, she couldn't imagine a better place to be. And to think she hadn't liked Christmas all these years. Guess it depended on who you celebrated with.

***

As Drew burrowed into Gina's hair, the soft scent of citrus filled his nose. "You smell good."

Gina wiggled in his lap as she settled closer. "I was going to meet you at the ranch. Mavis and Randi were supposed to keep you there."

"Guess they failed," he said with a grin. "I don't need an audience to tell you what I've got to say."

"They just let you go?" Before he could answer, her phone rang. She reached down and silenced it before setting in on the table. In a few seconds, it buzzed again. When they looked down, they saw Mavis on the caller ID. "Should I answer?"

"They'll keep calling until you do."

Gina swiped and hit the speaker. Mavis' voice filled the room. "Gina, we can't find him. He must have snuck out. Dex and Davie are going to hit the bars and bring him home."

Gina couldn't contain her laughter. "Tell them to stay home. He's here with me."

There was a moment of silence then some soft whispers Gina couldn't make out. Suddenly, they heard Randi. "Then our plan worked perfectly."

Gina snorted as Drew held her closer. "Your husbands might believe you set this up, but I don't. Lucky for you, Drew ended up right where he is supposed to be."

STEPHANIE BERGET

"It's a pretty safe bet you won't celebrate all of Christmas Eve with us, but we sure wish you'd come for a while. Nana Lucy is waiting for all her boys."

Drew took the phone. He didn't want to spend the next couple of hours talking to his sisters-in-law. "We've got things to do, but if Gina doesn't object, we'll be at the ranch in a couple of hours." He looked at her and she gave him a smile and a nod. "See you then."

"I was coming to see you."

"If I'd known that, it would have saved me a trip."

"You said we needed to talk. What's on your mind, cowboy?" Gina wrapped her arms around his neck.

He settled her onto the sofa beside him. Having her on his lap chased his thoughts away from what needed to be said. "First of all, I love you. I want you to know that."

Gina laid her hand against his cheek.

The soft skin of her fingertips stroked along his jawline.

When he opened his mouth to tell her he wasn't going to pressure her, she put her finger against his lips, silencing him. "I'm not the sharpest crayon in the box, but that's obvious." She smiled. "I think I fell in love with you the day you brought the Christmas tree, but I was afraid."

"Afraid of what? Me?"

She shook her head and gave a soft snort. "Of you, never. You are the kindest man I've ever met. I was afraid of what people would say, afraid of how you'd react to the gossip."

Even though he tried to remain expressionless, he felt his brows draw down.

She smoothed them out with a fingertip. "Many people in this town thought I loved Dex and when he married Mavis, they thought I was after Davie." She ran her hands through her hair, mussing the soft curls.

Drew ran his fingers through to smooth her hair. "I knew you weren't interested in them. You didn't have the look."

Now it was her turn to frown. "The look?"

This woman. She'd kept herself from loving or even getting close to anyone for the past years, and it was amazing to him that she'd been brave enough to love him. "You've seen Mavis and Randi look at my brothers. Even when they fought, they still had the look."

"And, I didn't have that look?"

"Not until I brought you the tree. The expression on your face changed, but I was afraid you wouldn't let yourself act on your feelings."

"I do love you, and no rumors or gossip will change that." Gina leaned close and gave him a soft kiss on the cheek.

He forced himself to relax. All he wanted was to lift her into his arms and carry her into the bedroom, but he had other news, and he felt it needed to be said. "My attorney called this afternoon. It appears Abbie's sugar daddy is tired of theatrics. He told her to either get a divorce or find someone else."

Gina's eyes widened. "Couldn't have happened to a nicer person."

"I guess the man laid down the law. Her lawsuit is off, and the divorce will be final the middle of January. I'll be a free man in a little over two weeks. I'll be your free man, if you'll have me." Drew dropped to one knee and took her hand. His heart pounded as he fished in his pocket. "I can't ask you to marry me yet, but will you be my steady girlfriend?" Slipping a ring on her finger, he leaned in for another kiss.

She glanced at the ring. Her laugh, soft and warm, caressed him. There wasn't a prettier sight in the world than Gina filled with happiness.

"How did you know this is the ring I dreamed of getting when I was a little girl?"

The Marvin the Martian cereal box ring gleamed dully in the light as she tilted her hand. "Marvin was my favorite." She dropped to her knees and took his hands in hers, twisting the left one so she could still see the ring. "I'd love to be your girlfriend. Does this mean I have to boot out my many boyfriends?"

"Yes, from this day forward, you're a one-man woman."

"I've been that for a while now."

His smile faded as he brought up the last, and most unpleasant thing he had to say. "You know Abbie is going to show up from time to time and cause trouble."

"I know."

Drew studied her. Something was different. Confidence shown from her eyes and all the indecision that always accompanied her was gone.

"I had a bit of an epiphany. I realized I'm the one who controls how I feel. Only me. I've spent most of my life trying to fit in and worrying about what people said about me. Heaven knows, my mom gave them enough gossip material." She wrapped her arms around him, pushing him to the floor before kissing him. "I'm not my mom."

"Yeah, I noticed that. Thank god." He tucked her beneath his arm and kissed her back.

She touched his cheek and sighed. "The townspeople can say anything they want. Abbie can do anything she wants, but as long as you love me, my life is perfect."

EPILOGUE

Gina spread the snowy white tablecloth on Lucy Dunbar's dining room table, smiling as she listened to Lucy hum in the kitchen. She'd had more family time in the six weeks since she'd given her heart to Drew than she'd had the rest of her life, doubled.

Lucy entered the room, her arms full of red lace. Handing one edge to Gina, they spread it over the table. Drew's grandmother straightened and put her hands on her hips. "That adds a little Valentine's Day spirit."

Gina traced the rose pattern with one finger as she smoothed the cloth. Glancing up, she saw Lucy doing the same thing. Her heart swelled with love for this old woman. Once Lucy truly believed Gina loved her grandson, the woman had welcomed her into the Dunbar family as if she'd been born into it. "This is lovely. Did you make it?"

"When the boys were little, Drew's mother, Miriam, asked me to teach her to crochet. She'd made a few doilies and was ready for something more complicated. After finding this pattern in a magazine, she decided to make it for Christmas. She completed about half before the accident." Lucy's hand covered her mouth, and she stared at nothing for a moment, lost in memories.

Gina waited. She knew Lucy and the boys' mother had been close.

"It sat in a box for years. I finally decided to finish it." Lucy's hands dropped to her hips. "It's yours to take home after dinner."

"Oh, I couldn't. It's yours."

"It was mine. I gave it to you." Lucy wrapped her arm around Gina's waist. "Miriam was going to make it out of white cotton thread, but she took Drew with her to buy the materials, and he insisted on red."

Gina gave her a squeeze. "Thank you. We'll treasure it."

"Now, girlie, help me put the dishes on the table. Everyone will be here soon."

As she followed Lucy into the kitchen, the old woman stopped and turned. Lucy put her hands around Gina's shoulders and gave her a hug. As she straightened, Gina noticed unshed tears in the woman's eyes. "Miriam would have loved you."

Before Gina could respond, the back door flew open and the Dunbar brothers and their wives filled the mud room. She swiped at her eyes, clearing the tears that had sprung up at the lovely compliment.

Drew dropped his boots to the floor and strode across the kitchen. He pulled Gina into his arms, and she felt the chill of the blustery winter day on his cheeks. "I think staying inside and helping your grandmother was a good decision on my part." She kissed his cold lips.

"Nah, it's a beautiful day."

"Yeah, if you like frozen fingers and toes," Randi complained as she stood over the furnace vent.

"Out of my way!" Mavis gently pushed at Dex then slid past him. "I get first dibs on the bathroom. No way was I going to make a pit stop out there." As she hurried down the hall, Gina heard the bathroom door shut.

"What did you and Nana do while we were gone?"

Drew sank on a dining room chair and pulled her onto his lap. "You're still alive, so I think your day must have gone well."

"What a thing to say. I love your grandmother."

"But you didn't always." He ran his fingers through her hair, and she sighed. The intimacy he took for granted still surprised her.

"I always thought your grandmother was special, the way she protected and loved you boys. She didn't feel the same about me, and I was jealous." Gina looked up as Lucy came back into the room.

"I needed to make sure you'd take care of my Drew," Lucy said. Her smile turned to a frown. "After that last woman... No, I won't let her ruin this celebration. The divorce is over, and we don't have to think of her again."

All three brothers looked at their grandmother.

"Celebration? What do you have up your sleeve, Nana?" Dex crossed the room and wrapped his arm around the old woman.

The back door opened then shut, and Rafe appeared in the kitchen doorway.

Nana Lucy rested her head against her grandson and smiled at the others. "I'm celebrating the fact that all my grandsons have found wonderful woman—and they've done it before I die."

"Hey, what about me? I haven't found a woman."

Nana pulled Rafe into a hug as Davie snorted and Drew laughed out loud.

"You're got time, Rafe. Nana Lucy will outlive all of us." Davie smiled.

Drew glanced at Gina. "First on the list is finding a good woman for Rafe then we'll need to start looking for a good man for Nana Lucy."

Lucy's cheeks glowed pink and with a huff, she hurried back into the kitchen.

Rafe shook his head. "Might be a tall order."

Dinner was a masterpiece of Lucy's ranch culinary

skills. When the table had been cleared and the dishes done, Lucy and Gina brought in the desserts they'd worked on while the rest of the Dunbar's checked the heifers.

Gina would never figure out why ranchers insisted on calving each year while snow still covered the landscape. She put the plate of heart shaped cookies on the table and selected one. Settling into the chair next to Drew, she handed it to him. "Your grandmother taught me how to bake her famous sugar cookies. Happy Valentine's Day." Not entirely comfortable with public displays of affection yet, she gave him a quick kiss on the cheek.

Drew raised the cookie to take a bite then stopped and read it. His laugh caught everyone's attention.

Gina felt the warmth of a blush color her cheeks.

"That must be some cookie if it makes Gina blush," Randi said with a giggle. "I might have to learn how to cook."

There had been a time when Gina would have taken offence, when she would have looked for Randi's nasty hidden meaning. Finally, she was learning to trust these people. "It's silly."

With every pair of eyes on them, Drew shrugged. "If Gina says wants it to be kept private, it'll be private."

"Oh, go on and tell them." She relaxed into her chair. She'd found the family she'd always yearned for, and she was enjoying every minute.

Drew looked at each person in turn as if what he had to say was of great importance. He held it up for everyone to see. In white frosting script were the words, *Will you be my steady boyfriend?*

Laughter broke out, and it took a few minutes for them to calm down. When everyone was busy choosing a cookie and accepting the hot cider Nana Lucy offered, Drew stood and rapped a spoon on his cup. "I have a cookie for Gina, too. Only mine won't taste as good."

He pulled something out of his pocket and dropped to

one knee.

Gina heard Mavis gasp and Randi's soft whoop, but her gaze was locked on Drew.

As he tipped up the top of the small dark blue velvet box, it was Gina's turn to gasp. Black and white diamonds formed two matching swirls edged in gold. It was understated elegance, and Gina couldn't think of anything she'd like better.

She looked at the man she loved and didn't fight the tears. "Yes, yes, so much yes."

"I didn't ask you yet." Drew laughed, but when she reached for the ring, he held it out of her reach. "Take it easy there, Wally. I want to do this right."

He took her left hand in his. "Gina Wallace, will you marry me?"

She nodded. For the moment, the power of speech deserted her.

He slipped the ring on her finger. "This is your engagement ring. I was going to surprise you, but I can't wait. Do you want to see the wedding ring?"

When she nodded again, he reached into his pocket and pulled out a thin gold band.

Laughter and happiness bubbled out of her, and she laced the fingers of her free hand through his.

Drew picked up the ring and held it where she could get a better look. "I ordered this the day after Christmas. I picked it up yesterday, just in time for our Valentine's celebration."

She squinted and leaned closer. Not only did this man love her, he understood her.

Where the top of the ring widened was a tiny detailed engraving of Marvin the Martian head. A black diamond created the cartoon character's face.

"Do you like it?" Drew's smile had faded as he watched her study the ring. "We can pick out another one if you want."

"I love it, and I love you, Drew Dunbar." The words

she'd found so hard to say for so long now flowed out of her heart. She couldn't have stopped them if she tried. Leaning closer, she kissed her Dunbar brother.

"You are forever mine." Drew tucked a wisp of hair behind her ear. "Forever."

"You are mine for forever and a day." She held out her hand and studied her ring. "Marvin the Martian will make sure of that."

Romance Beneath A Rodeo Moon

If you enjoyed reading Saving A Cowboy's Christmas, you can find more of the cowboys and cowgirls in the Rodeo Road Series, beginning with Changing A Cowboy's Tune, featuring the oldest brother Dex and his high school sweetheart, Mavis.

Three years and a thousand miles... Hasn't been far enough.

He climbed out of the truck, and she forced a smile. Fake it to make it, right? She only hoped the charade worked this time, because he knew her secrets, and he knew her fantasies.

She'd thought he knew her heart.

Boy, had she been wrong.

The time on the rodeo road should have eased her desire, but his clear blue eyes and wicked smile, not to mention the way he filled out a T-shirt, made her rethink the years she'd spent alone. On the way home, she'd told herself she could handle seeing him again.

Yet, another thing she'd been wrong about.

Because, the bronc rider was her kryptonite.

If you like Western Romances with strong women and determined cowboys, you'll love _Changing A Cowboy's Tune._

Changing A Cowboy's Tune-Get your copy today!

For more cowboy romance, check out my Sugar Coated Cowboys series. Book one is _Gimme Some Sugar._

Gimme Some Sugar-Pastry chef, Cary Crockett, is on the run. Pursued by a loan shark bent on retrieving gambling debts owed him by her deadbeat ex-boyfriend, she finds the perfect hiding place at the remote Circle W Ranch. More at home with city life, cupcakes and croissants than beef, beans and bacon, she has to convince ranch owner Micah West she's up to the job of feeding his hired hands. The overwhelming attraction she feels toward him was nowhere in the job description.

Micah West has a big problem. The camp-cook on his central Oregon ranch has up and quit without notice, and his crew of hungry cowboys is about to mutiny. He agrees to hire Cary on a temporary basis, just until he finds the right man to fill the job. Maintaining a hands-off policy toward his sexy new cook becomes tougher than managing a herd of disgruntled wranglers.

Gimme Some Sugar

Gimme Some Sugar Excerpt

Snapping his head up, he whirled around, almost elbowing the woman standing behind him. Pulling in a deep, slow breath, partly to gather some semblance of calm and partly to adjust to the tingle where her hand met his arm, he took a step back before speaking.

"Help me with what?" Did he know her? He was sure he didn't, but man....

"I'm sorry. I didn't mean to eavesdrop, but I heard you say you're looking for a cook." Golden eyes the color of whiskey stared into his. "I cook."

He let his gaze wander over her, liking what he saw. She wasn't a local. Her white blond hair was as short as a man's on the sides and curled longer on the top and back. He hadn't seen any woman, or anyone at all who wore their hair like this. Of course, tastes of the people of East Hope ran to the conservative.

Despite the severe hairstyle, she was pretty. Beyond pretty. Leather pants showed off her soft curves, miniature combat boots encased her small feet and a tight tank top enhanced her breasts.

When she cleared her throat, he jerked his eyes up to

her face. "It won't do you any good to talk to my breasts. Like most women, it's my brain that answers questions."

A smart ass and she'd caught him red-handed. His cheeks warmed. Damn it, he was blushing. This woman was not at all what he needed. Time to end this. "I have a ranch, the Circle W. We need a camp cook. A man."

Her eyes narrowed, and her body tensed. "It looks like you need any kind of cook you can get." She held her hand out, indicating the empty café. "Not a lot of takers."

She had him there. His gut told him he was going to regret this, but she was right. He had no choice. "I'll hire you week to week." When she nodded, he continued. "I've got seven ranch hands. You'll cook breakfast and dinner and pack lunches, Monday through Friday and serve Sunday dinner to the hands who are back by six o'clock."

She bounced on the toes of her feet until she noticed him watching her then she pulled on a cloak of calm indifference. "You won't regret this."

He felt a smile touch the corners of his mouth as his gut twisted. "I already do."

Gimme Some Sugar

Last, But Not Least, Is My *Harney County Cowboys Series.*

Book one is Tied To A Dream

No more cowboys...
Or western knights-in-shining-armor...
Not even the Marlboro Man himself!
Being alone has taught Frannie O'Connell to be self-sufficient, but being Superwoman is harder than it looks.

She's pulling an all-night drive to reach her next rodeo. It's past midnight on a lonely mountain road, and if she doesn't catch a few winks, there's a better than average chance she'll run her rig into the river.

Her barrel racing dreams are interrupted when a stranger knocks on her truck's window.

He's a cowboy by the looks of his black Stetson and tight Wranglers. But what's the man doing out here? His deep blue eyes and sexy smile have her reaching for the door handle when her brain finally takes control.

Her mama taught her manners, and her daddy taught her to be tough. But, her brother and her ex pounded home the fact that not everyone is trustworthy.

His offer of aid is tempting. She knows being safe is better than sorry, but he'd helped her earlier at the rodeo.

Sometimes a cowgirl has to go with her gut.

You'll love this contemporary rodeo romance, because love isn't always blind.

Get your copy today. http://bit.ly/TiedToADream

ABOUT THE AUTHOR

Stephanie Berget was born loving horses, a ranch kid trapped in a city girl's body. It took her twelve years to convince her parents she needed a horse of her own. She found her way to rodeo when she married her own hot cowboy. She and the Bronc Rider traveled throughout the Northwest while she ran barrels and her cowboy rode bucking horses. She started writing to put a realistic view of rodeo and ranching into western romance. Stephanie and her husband live on a farm, located along the Oregon/Idaho border. They raise hay, horses and cattle, with the help of Dizzy Dottie, the Border Collie and Cisco, barrel and team roping horse extraordinaire.

Stephanie is delighted to hear from readers. Reach her at http://www.stephanieberget.com
Facebook:
https://www.facebook.com/stephaniebergetwrites/
Amazon: Stephanie Berget

Made in United States
North Haven, CT
20 May 2022

19340158R00064